BROWSING COLLECTION
14-DAY CHECKOUT
No Holds • No Renewals

Land

of

Milk

and

Honey

ALSO BY C PAM ZHANG

How Much of These Hills Is Gold

Land
of
Milk
and
Honey

C PAM ZHANG

RIVERHEAD BOOKS

NEW YORK

2023

RIVERHEAD BOOKS
An imprint of Penguin Random House LLC
penguinrandomhouse.com

Images on pages 45, 91, 149, and 217 were generated by
the author using the DALL-E 2 AI system

Library of Congress Cataloging-in-Publication Data

Names: Zhang, C Pam, author.
Title: Land of milk and honey / C Pam Zhang.
Description: New York : Riverhead Books, 2023.
Identifiers: LCCN 2022045590 (print) | LCCN 2022045591 (ebook) |
ISBN 9780593538241 (hardcover) | ISBN 9780593538265 (ebook)
ISBN 9780593715871 (international edition)
Subjects: LCGFT: Novels.
Classification: LCC PS3626.H35 L36 2023 (print) |
LCC PS3626.H35 (ebook) | DDC 813/.6—dc23
LC record available at https://lccn.loc.gov/2022045590
LC ebook record available at https://lccn.loc.gov/2022045591

International edition ISBN: 9780593715871

Printed in the United States of America
1st Printing

Book design by Alexis Farabaugh

For Spike and Bagu

ONE DAY, after my life is already over, a girl comes up to me at the back of the auditorium and says, *Are you the famous chef from Miele?* The question does not surprise me so much as the asker. She is eighteen or nineteen at most, with a face that has not quite grown into its bones, has not decided what it means to be, ferocious or mild, pretty or something more. She is young to be concerned with a period of time that her generation prefers to forget—that my generation would forget if not for the ruptures that open up in our sleep, that gnawing.

I know you, she says, and I look at her again. She is nothing like the other, except that I was wrong about her youth. Not her age: her youth. Beneath that soft skin is an attitude older, implacable as rock, so that she commands the space of the now-empty auditorium. Other conversations leak from the corridor: last week's class, which salad spot for lunch, dull, ordinary, a world apart. *Did you know what would happen before you left the country?* Her questions come faster with my pulse. *You must have known about the parts, didn't you?—escape because—know they would die.*

I find the words at last. They are there, alive. How to explain it all. How to begin. At the beginning: I say, *I was just some mediocre cook.*

And then my breath fails me, I wheeze, those words a hook in my chest, and I am slipping my old woman's skin as if it is costume; I am sloughing this room, this soil, this year; I am back to that place very high and very far where I can't speak for the thinness of crisp, mountain air.

Back to that country that no longer exists. That country that was mine for a year in the sun.

One

⚜

I fled to that country because I would have gone anywhere, done anything, for one last taste of green sharp enough to pierce the caul of my life. I was twenty-nine, a hungry ghost, adrift. I hadn't seen California in ten years, hadn't tasted a strawberry or a leaf of lettuce in three. Hunger was simple, as the rest was not.

Here is the rest: I was an American stranded in England when America's borders closed; I was a cook as that profession lay dying. Both troubles shared one source, namely the smog that spread from a cornfield in Iowa and soon occluded the sun, smothering as it went fields of wheat in Canada and paddies of hard yellow rice in Peru. No more lemon trees fragrant on the slopes of Greece, no more sugarcane striping Vietnam, no more small, sweet Indian mangos. Biodiversity fell. Wildlife and livestock perished for lack of feed. Scientists bickered over the smog's composition and politicians over whether pollution or lax carbon taxes or China or nuclear testing or America or Russia were to blame, and all the while the darkness, slightly acidic, ate its way through fertile fields. America plunged into famine while my career hung suspended by the sea—the wrong sea, the oily, inhospitable Atlantic. Each morning I walked to the American consulate to hear the demurral, *Soon*. Each afternoon I thawed frozen fish at the restaurant that underwrote my refugee visa. My life was dredge, fry, plate. My life was wait, wait, wait.

The day the letter arrived for me from California was the day the chef announced pesto cut from the menu for good. No more nuts and seeds in the pantry, and no basil, not even the powdered kind. I barely heard. I took my envelope into the walk-in freezer, as if ice might cool desire.

With my back against chilled steel, I extracted not an American re-entry permit but a bill. The letter informed me that my dead mother's apartment in Los Angeles had burned down. *Regrettable accident*, the lawyer wrote of the riot that caused it, and then, *legally liable*. Cataloged in detail were waste disposal fees and firefighting fees and city emissions fines, but nowhere did the bill mention the color of the apartment walls, which I no longer recalled. No avocados, no strawberries, no almonds. California had become a food desert and I imagined wind howling through broken windows, scouring, dry, unclean.

The door opened as I was doing the math. *Chef says break's over*, a line cook told me. *He wants you to make a sub for the pesto.*

With what?

The cook kicked a bag of flour on his way out. *Anything you want, princess, so long as you use this shit.*

The flour puffed up in a fine gray cloud. No parsley, no sage, no produce of any sort. It was spring. March. But a false spring in which crops would fail for the third year running. Blame the smog's acidity, as some did, or anhydrites, or a lack of sun and morality—what it amounted to was skies that were gray and kitchens that were gray. You could taste it: gray. No olives, no quails, no grapes of the tart green kind for Champagne. I took stock of the restaurant's dwindling supplies:

dusty tins, icy slabs of years-old fish. Mostly it was bag after bag of the mung-protein-soy-algal flour distributed by the government.

We were lucky to have it! they said. The flour was a miracle of nutritional science, engineered from plants that tolerated dark. Lucky that the smog had taken a year and a half to reach Europe, lucky we'd escaped the famine that ravaged the Americas and Southeast Asia, lucky that mung-protein flour was calorie for calorie cheaper than the cobbled-together diets of old. Yet the flour was gritty and gray, and the bread it baked could not be coaxed to rise. I am speaking of an occlusion in my twenty-ninth year, a dimming of how far I could see in front of me; I am speaking not only of the air.

Chef had lost its meaning, like *lucky*, like *fresh*, like *soon*. No saffron, no buffalo, no polished short-grain rice. Dishes winked out from menus like extinguished stars as a conservative, nativist attitude seized the few restaurants that remained open thanks to government subsidies. As they shut borders to refugees, so countries shut their palates to all but those cuisines deemed essential. In England, the shrinking supplies of frozen fish were reserved for kippers, or gray renditions of cod and chips—and, of course, a few atrociously expensive French preparations with which a diner might buy, along with sour wine, the illusion that she still lived in luxury. Back to stodgy safety. Back to national dishes unchanged for centuries. The loss of pesto should have come as no surprise in a world with no favas, no milkfish, no Curry Lane in London or Thai Town in LA, no fusion, no specials of the day, no truffles turned out like sheepish lovers from under their blankets of sod. We were lucky, those around me said. We survived.

But in the dimness of that refrigerated room I could no longer see a future for the halibut dish without pesto, as I could not fathom the depth of my debt, or the tint of cloudless sky. Couldn't see what it was for which I survived. I was alien to the Brits with their stiff upper lips; if I had a friend in that dank port town, it was the drunk who haunted the half-empty market, proclaiming the end of everything.

That day, I knew. A world was gone. Goodbye to all that, to the person I'd been, to she who'd abandoned, half-eaten, a plate of carnitas under blaze of California sun. It wasn't grease I missed so much as the revelation of lime. Waiting on grief, I met hunger. For radish, radicchio, the bitter green of endive.

And so I quit that job to pursue recklessly, immorally, desperately, the only one that gave me hope of lettuce. The position was private chef for what advertised itself as an *elite research community* on a minor mountain at the Italian-French border. A quick search turned up that controversy. The community's objective was to bioengineer food crops capable of withstanding smog, all discoveries to be shared with the Italian government—but because funding came from private investors, to strike the deal parliament had ceded one of the rare high-elevation zones still blessed by occasional sunlight. And so the mountain was populated by investors and their attendant scientists, staff, medics, field hands, et cetera who enjoyed carte blanche when it came to how they met their lofty research goals. Apart from quarterly check-ins by the Italian ministry of agriculture, there were no monitors, no police presence, no communications out or in: the mountain governed itself with diplomatic immunity. The howling online was murderous. *A beast who is fat may buy his own country!!* I read in one of the auto-translated comments, which confused me until I looked up an alternate translation: *Rich monster.*

All that mattered to me was the job's promise of fresh produce, but—here was the catch—no guarantee of a long-term visa. It was a ten-week contract-to-hire. At-will employment, at my employer's will.

Colleagues at the seafood restaurant inquired after my sanity when I resigned. They reminded me of the thousands begging for my work visa.

I wasn't unaware of the risk. It was for this reason that I supplemented my application with lies. The job called for a formally educated, French-trained chef capable of *working with unusual ingredients* and *turning out exquisite haute cuisine*, and so I hammed up my experience. Education at Le Cordon Bleu in Paris, sous chef at a Michelin-starred restaurant that closed when its owner was found hanged from a string of her own saucissons—no one to refute my claim. If I hesitated at my lies, or at the extreme isolation the community demanded (nondisclosure agreement, no phone, no internet, no contact, no family, no leaving restaurant grounds without permission)—if I hesitated at my younger self's declaration that everyone would taste my food, that cooking was an art neither frivolous nor selfish—well. I was no longer she who'd left California with scruples and ambition; as I did not know who I was, exactly, I molded myself to the application's shape.

Only at the end of the form did I concede to honesty. *I am your perfect candidate*, I wrote in the open text field, *because I have nowhere on earth to return to. I will faithfully perform any task within reason, and with dignity.*

Possibly this was insane. It's true that my sole confidant before leaving England was the supermarket drunk. *You understand*, I whispered, *I have to do this.* His breath, as he kissed my palm, had the antiseptic coolness of mung-protein flour. Shoppers gave us wide berth. They lied to themselves, as scientists lied, as politicians lied, as my employer with his opacity and his dubious wealth must have lied, too. I only cared that he provide a head of shriveled lettuce; even iceberg would do. That was my wish. That was my fantasy.

I first began to sense something beyond the dusty rim of the plate I called my life when I received my acceptance. There was no further clarification of my duties. Just one sheet of thick, expensive paper that gave off a hint of citrus, plus a scent I couldn't name, grassy and sweet. On the front was the location where I'd be picked up by private jet. On the back, a handwritten note. *I, too, am a dignified man*, my employer wrote, *a fact you will see for yourself.*

And so I crossed into the land of milk and honey knowing nothing, not even the country's true name. It was the officer at the Italian border who first said, *Terra di latte e miele?*

It was three in the morning. I'd flown through the night and could not quite see where I'd landed, nor my interrogator's face. The hatred in his voice was so intimate that I wondered if I knew him.

No thanks, I don't want coffee, I said, latching to the one word I thought I understood. I understood nothing, my god.

I hadn't encountered that odd, archaic phrase before my arrival; I wasn't meant to. They hid the country's true name as they hid its true nature. After Italian immigration, it was the mountain's private security that held me for hours, taking my passport, my retina scans, the measurements of my face and waist and earlobes, my blood, my phone, my photo. This last made the guard pause for so long that I grew nervous. The picture I'd sent with my application was slightly blurred, taken from a distance, my features indistinct. As if, should I be discovered, I might plausibly deny being myself.

The guard touched her throat. ——— ——— —————— ——, she said, and let me pass.

It was in the small hours of morning that I drove up the mountain in a discreet black car. The wind nipped, hard, and though the air up high was smogless, it was cheerless, too. Rocks scrawled gloomy warnings in the dark. Occasionally a compound would loom, then vanish, in a flash of high, cold wall that seemed intent on excluding me—an impression that proved correct, because never would I be invited into the homes and private lives of those investors. The piece of mountain I claim is heat and toil, soft flesh and the hard taste of salt.

What fields I passed were sere and dead. No sign of spring, for all my employer's grandiose goals. I'd pared my expectations down to dried herbs by the time I reached the mountain's peak.

The restaurant at the top appeared as a hulking box the same dark hue as the sky it rose against. No windows broke the monotony of those walls. A cliff behind dropped into abyss and the front lawn, while vast, was muddy. I found the lights off, no answer at the locked door. I shivered, perplexed, as the sky lightened.

The door clicked open at last. I stepped through just as sun rose over the mountain.

Much later it would occur to me that he had timed this moment, my employer with his flair for the dramatic, a man who named his country with a prophet's arrogance. The light was stunning, transcendent, a white-hot bullet between the eyes. From behind my fingers I saw dark walls blush lavender, orange, pink. The restaurant was built of two-way glass, opaque from without and transparent from within, so that on my first morning I had the impression of no walls, no windows, no doors, just the suspension of my body in sky, sky, sky, sky, sky. I had traveled, it seemed, through those low, smoggy years to emerge in this vessel of light.

I would come to know the restaurant in its many moods. Blue by day, apricot at sunset, bruised by the advent of night or storm. The view never ceased to awe. All the rest of my time I'd experience headaches, mild vertigo, a kind of drunkenness on the light that gilded the dining rooms, and pooled on the bed in the suite labeled EMPLOYEES ONLY, and made a blaze of the chef's coats I found in the closet, along with a white silk dress, floor-length, some housekeeper's mistake.

The kitchen was the room most loved by light. Sun streamed down and made the white appliances one continuous pour of milk. I wanted to lick it; I settled for touch. I strummed the marble counters and turned dials on the twelve-range stove, and when I ran a hand over the back-splash I discovered under my fingers ivory suede, an insane material, impossible to keep clean, but so plush it held my imprint. As I stood at the window counting the Tiffany fish knives, I felt a euphoria such as the first European colonizers must have upon sighting new land. *Mine*, I thought, and it wasn't for a while that I realized the kitchen was empty of food.

On my second pass, I spotted a box behind the door. *Impress me*, this note said. Inside were flour, vanilla, eggs.

I'd expected a test, of course: a textbook omelet, or a flawless con-sommé to prove the French training the job demanded. Pastry, no. Giddiness abandoned me as I unpacked baking soda, sugar, milk. Even the voluptuousness of the butter couldn't distract from thoughts of my spotty experience in pâtisserie, and the precarity of my visa, and what would happen were I turned away—and then I was no longer thinking because at the bottom of the box I touched something as warm as skin, as yielding as a woman's inner thigh: strawberries.

Amen, I heard myself say, wet-mouthed. I was surprised my breath didn't smudge the air. Red: that color of desire. I began again and said the whole prayer, *Our Father* through *daily bread*. Not my words. They belonged to a pastry chef I'd loved, a lapsed Catholic who re-discovered his faith each morning as he fingered the day's shipment of fruit, and forgot it anew each afternoon as we fucked among the butter and jam. He was the first to take seriously my appetites, my ambitions. He never stored a strawberry cold. Close to the stem, he said, closest to the earth, their perfume is complex, not sugar: closer to flesh, the flesh of a loved one, not sanitized, not anodyne, but full of many waters. Strawberries and spring, strawberries and musk, strawberries and sex flooded back as I crushed my tongue to sugar. I'd come to that country hardly daring for bitter green and here, now, this rupturing sweet-ness. I couldn't remember what hour it was, how many time zones I'd crossed, when I'd last eaten. For years I'd fed, survived, swallowed my portions of gray—but had I hungered for pleasure?

Go light, light, light, said the pastry chef. *Not too hard, the touch.* So I simmered the fruit with sugar. Eased together a batter, barely stirring. The shortcakes came whispering from the oven, pale mounds, uncom-promised. I slipped fingers into their heat. Outside the grass was scant and dead and below my pane of mountain sky, smog clung to the low-lands like scum on stock, one unending gray season. But on my tongue it was summer and it was spring and seasons flourished and vines ran high. Butter and fruit: my mouth an orchard in the sun.

I lowered the heat to a simmer and waited for my compote to cook down. Even waiting was sweet, the exquisite and long-forgotten flush of desire, withheld, licking through me as I waited to learn how what I made would be received.

When I woke it was dark and my neck spasmed from sleeping at the base of the stove. Night had fallen, fallen down. The air smelled scorched, evil. Calmly I understood that I must be in hell, that the clear sky, kitchen, fruit had been a dream of the dead. I was where I deserved to be: burnt to a crisp in Los Angeles.

I stood. The compote had reduced to black tar. Someone had switched off the stove. My shortcakes were gone, and I stumbled to the door to see a car reversing down the drive.

Wait, I called. Wind stole my breath. *What do I do now?* The car was turning, departing, and suddenly a great desolation filled my lungs, black and stiff, and I lost all sense of dignity as I ran headlong down the drive, screaming as I hadn't screamed when I read the lawyer's letter, loud enough to make my vision flicker as I flung my voice across that strange country, *Now, now, now now now.*

An arm emerged from the car. Broad shoulders, a pale suit. My employer—I knew it must be him—flung an object into the dark. It was a shortcake. More pattered down. He did not taste them that I saw. And I saw, through that impossibly crisp mountain air that freezes each detail in pitiless clarity, one black eye. It was not a man's eye, not at all. It was the eye of a sturgeon or a shark, those deepwater creatures of the cold whose forms have remained unchanged for millions of years, static through the fracturing of eons. It was an eye to outlast the end of the world, and I still think of it with amazement; I still think that despite all evidence, an eye like that cannot be kept dead. The car disappeared from view. I fought to breathe. Above me the first stars were white ashes scattered over the burnt-black sky. The yolk of the moon throbbed, broken. Never had everything seemed so close and so far.

I trailed him to the fence. There I waited, dumb, shivering, impotent. The contract was clear: I was not to leave restaurant grounds without approval.

Not that I believed the contract would stand much longer. The kitchen smoked with my failure when I returned. My guts cramped at the idea of being sent back, the descent and then the flight and then the numbing taste of mung-protein flour that could sustain a body for decades, containing as it did the requisite nutrients, that could make the days go on and go on and go on. I pressed my forehead to the cold glass. Out there was the cliff, the drop; the cool, analgesic wind of that much swifter descent. My stomach clenched.

For the second time, I tasted strawberries.

When I say I grew up in Los Angeles I mean that I grew up in a constellation of little-known satellite towns at the center of which Los Angeles—glitz, Hollywood, beach-toned blondes—revolves. In Pasaje, California, my mother and I lived by fields of lettuce and strawberries and almonds that fed the dream. In picking season the growers paid extra for every pair of hands, and so if money was tight, if my mother took on night shifts at the nursing home, then she, too, could join the migrant laborers in the rows. In picking season we ate for weeks like the wealthy, bushel after bushel of prime fruit. It was economical. Strawberries and syrup, strawberries and rice, strawberries in vinegar and chilies and oil, as juice as mash as soup, strawberries eaten to excess in a race against the burning, punishing springs during which workers fell to heatstroke and the sun was a terror not a dream, and still they sprayed the field with pesticides and clawed what they could from the land until it dried, and withered, ready to burst into flame. Strawberries sat abandoned in the fields by season's end, so ripe as to be barely solid, warm as heart's blood. Ambrosia, they call that variety, the food of gods. But the hubris of excess has mortal consequences. You can go blind, mad, drown in red. The second nature of strawberries is a sugar that turns to rot.

They reappeared one by one as I vomited, shapeless and no longer sweet, those little, used, red hearts.

I found a new note waiting in the EMPLOYEES ONLY suite, an intrusion into space that was not, had never been, mine. *Prepare eight courses for two on Sunday evening. The full extent of your abilities will be evaluated then.*

Scribbled at the bottom, so hard the pen had broken through: *Do not burn my restaurant down.*

There followed a menu, and instructions for accessing the storeroom. I inhaled from the page, but whatever scent I'd hoped to find was gone. With fingers blue from cold I held my employer's warning against a lamp, over flame, up to the full-length mirror in the bathroom. No secret message appeared. Only my own pale face.

And beyond it—

I groped behind the glass. Felt empty space. Both arms straining, I pushed until the mirror slid aside to admit me into a hidden room.

Even now I see it as an eye. It bulges, glassy, from the back of the restaurant; through the years, it watches me. I see myself crawl into that convex, ovoid space. I note the round briefcase that rests like an iris against the curve. I see myself seeing, through the glass beneath my knees, a sheer drop into abyss below. I backed out in a hurry.

Two

⚜

Each morning of that first week I rose, smoked a contraband cigarette or four to quell my nerves, opened windows to air out the smell, and then, adrenalized by nicotine and fear, I worked to validate my continued existence.

I'm five foot one. My voice is not loud; my disposition in a group, I'm told, seems yielding. I was no stranger to proving my worth in kitchens where I'd chopped faster and worked longer than men who sang out *honey, sweetheart, bitch*. I'd inked my arms and, once, shaved my head to deliver the warning my stature could not. My chosen career was one of trials and thankless grind, but never was an audition so desperate as the one I performed in that country, nor so eerie.

The storeroom lay beneath a kitchen counter the precise pink of raw chicken. Like all expensive marble, it shone as if perpetually moist. In certain lights the counter appeared to pulse, like a lung or spleen. Or, lifting open, a tongue that made way to the restaurant's belly.

One hundred and fifty-six pink steps led down. No elevator. The risk of a broken neck was, I guess, a part of the drama. Sconces lit and darkened as I passed. Each time, I was seized by a fear that the steps might never end, that I descended into an underworld with no hope of return. Not for me, spring.

At the bottom of the passage, behind thick steel doors, I witnessed the true wealth of that country.

Others have estimated the value in those rooms of grains, of nuts, of beans; of the millions in canned foie and white asparagus; of the greenhouses under their orange lights, and the vast spice grottos. I can't quote numbers. I can only say what happened when I pressed my face to a wheel of ten-year Parmigiano, how in a burst of grass and ripe pineapple I stood in some green meadow that existed only in the resonance, like a bell's fading peal, of that aroma. I can tell you how it was to cradle wines and vinegars older than myself, their labels crying out the names of lost traditions. And I can tell you of the ferocious crack in my heart when I walked into the deep freezer to see chickens, pigs, rabbits, cows, pheasants, tunas, sturgeon, boars hung two by two. No more boars roamed the world above, no Öland geese, no sharks; the day I climbed the mountain, there vanished the wild larks. I knew, then, why the storerooms were guarded as if they held gold, or nuclear armaments. They hid something rarer still: a passage back through time.

The animal carcasses were left unskinned. In the circulating air, the extinct revolved on their hooks to greet me.

That was the closest I came to encountering a living creature of the mountain in my first week. My phone sat in a vault at the border, and the restaurant, for all its gleaming modernity, lacked computers and hooked-up TVs. Just one landline labeled FOR EMERGENCY USE. No diners, either, and no staff, though each morning the kitchen had been scrubbed clean. One day I laced my shoes and took the stairs at a sprint, just in time to glimpse a figure in the storeroom, fleeing. The woman looked back as she passed through a door labeled RESTRICTED: AUTHO- RIZED STAFF ONLY. There was terror on her brown face.

I'd read the fairy tales and knew better than to seek forbidden rooms, which did not, in any case, respond to my retina scan. Still, I couldn't shake the idea that the staff member had seen, behind me, some mon- strosity I was blind to.

I came to feel an unease seemingly at odds with the gracious rooms, the bountiful ingredients, the languid spread of sun through the length- ening hours of the day. At some point, those qualities themselves be- came the root of my unease. At night, sounds acquired a sinister texture as they bounced off vaulted ceilings. The too-copious sun made me feel observed, a specimen under glass. And the food—well.

My employer's first menu included such items as steak tartare, vichys- soise, seared foie with port wine reduction, lobster thermidor, rack of lamb, mousse au chocolat. As if he'd stabbed randomly at a French cookbook written for American housewives of the previous century: *Im- press your friends and make yourself the envy of enemies!* Despite its vast store of ingredients, my employer's restaurant defaulted, like others in that age, to familiar symbols of prestige. French classics with lots of cream, lots of butter, expensive ingredients, just money glopped on the plate. Money. In refining recipes for the trial dinner, I threw out vats of demiglace, kilos of filet, a king's ransom in terrine, marrow, porcini. The waste felt criminal. But I couldn't eat the food myself.

What happened with the strawberries repeated when I sat down to a rib eye, richly crusted, or buttered onions sweet as gems. Even an egg yolk made me gag. And so I found myself drinking black coffee and gnawing ginger. Dry bread, boiled rice. For a treat I might paint turnips with corbezolo honey, which tastes less of sugar than tannin, leather, ash. And though I ate through pounds of radicchio and escarole, though I was awash in chicories, even those never, quite, satisfied my appetite. It was bitterness my palate craved, a desire unrecognizable to me, as the woman who stared back from the restaurant's many reflective surfaces was unrecognizable. The light, uncompromising, revealed dark circles. Flat exhaustion. A mouth grown thinner, harsher, changed.

I told myself this was my body's natural reaction to the deprivation of recent years. Something to do with recouping vitamins and minerals. Something like the way pregnant women find themselves drinking vinegar and chewing chalk; or the shipwrecked who, after rescue, require small meals. My appetite must come back.

And yet. After tastings from my employer's menu, guts roiling with cream and questions of my future, I found myself craving a dab, a pinch, just a soupçon of mung-protein flour. That metallic tang, like medicine. Without my knowing, it had grown familiar—a link, as I floated alone through days of terrifying uncertain abundance, to the world of gray plates and empty shelves, of starving children in Louisville and Addis Ababa. I imagined small faces pressed against the glass as they watched me throw out pounds of pommes dauphine. The sameness of the smog, it occurred to me, had also felt safe: it was unchanging.

The cat, to confound me, outdid my picky eating.

I had a cat in those days. Not mine—my dead mother's. He was a small black creature, thick-furred and disconsolate, and we didn't like one another much. I'd expected my employer to refuse the cat and received this cryptic encouragement: *Greater biodiversity is always wel-*

come. And so the burden I'd acquired at nineteen came up the mountain, too.

I'd taken the cat when I stormed from my mother's home to begin what I believed to be a grand culinary career. I took the cat and abandoned my premed textbooks, when I should have sold the books and I always meant to return the cat. But then came the opportunity in upstate New York, and Lyon, and Paris, and the avian flu that kept Europe under quarantine, and the smog, and mutual resentment, pride, closed borders, and here we were. We'd all known—she, me, cat— that his place should have been beside my mother. Wherever I dragged him in my nomadic career he never, quite, fit; at each new stop he hated the roommate or shredded the couch, or yowled at midnight in protest of the radiator's clank. He became an escape artist. Was forever baiting dogs and drinking from puddles that led to inevitable bouts of diarrhea. His was a sensitive stomach allergic to most packaged pet foods; in the end, I cooked for him and locked him up for his own safety, an act he repaid by peeing on my shoes. Like I said, not a pleasant creature. When my mother died—sudden heart failure, weak valves—the cat seemed to know. The day of the hospital's call, he bolted free only to slump, disoriented, mere feet beyond the door. He returned, with obvious reluctance, to me.

He made it clear, in short, that I was a perpetual disappointment. If my eating habits grew peculiar on the mountain, his were outright sadistic. I was driven frantic by his refusal of chicken, fresh milk, salmon bellies, mashed and marinated quail eggs, partridge, abalone, elk. In my darkest moments I believed his hunger strike was mockery of the kind his previous owner had employed, another way to dismiss my profession as unskilled labor, another way of saying that what I did would never be good enough. The cat lost weight. The sight of his ribs was an insult that cut off my breath, made me yell and yell.

We reached a détente when he escaped to an abandoned security post down in the storeroom. It held an ancient TV, and a dusty collection of DVDs and books, plus a live feed of the restaurant's front door. There I left the cat to his own devices. Some days I'd wake up and forget he existed: his surliness, his judgment. Some days I'd wake into sunshine so obliterating it was as if a nuclear detonation had gone off in the night and wiped out the world, nothingness advancing bit by bit till I, too, would cease to exist, and that was wonderful.

Anyway, once I realized that the sun continued its merciless yank across the sky, I hauled beef or crème fraîche or tarragon up from the storeroom and began to cook. I practiced for the trial meal like a gladiator about to meet the lion: grimly, stomach in knots, knowing my life depended on it. Gagging on jus so sticky it coated my tonsils, jabbing a knife between a lobster's bright, ball bearing eyes, I said, to quell my nausea, *I'm supposed to be a chef.*

On Sunday I changed my outfit twice, a pointless vanity. My uniforms were indistinguishable, meant to make their wearer disappear. Not so the car that drove in.

I watched a candy-apple-red convertible rocket up the drive. Gravel spat from its tires, which left the road, twice. A fence post fell as the vehicle screeched to a stop.

The young woman who emerged was just as unnerving. Shaggy furs above, stick legs below, with the slight stagger of a bird blown off course and stranded thousands of miles from its destination. No—as I watched her cross that brown field, her body bent into angles against the wind, I thought it wasn't miles but light-years, that she must be an apparition from a future on a barren planet. As she came close I saw the four-inch stilettos responsible for her gait, and the lipstick the same red as her coat, and the small nose, and the freckles so numerous they ran together in fat blotches like caramel stirred through cream. Her eyes were black and lively.

She entered without knocking. In flawless British English she said, *My father promised me the very best French chef.*

I was stunned into truth. *He lied.*

The girl reared back. A break, a shatter, a yowl from beneath that polished surface: she laughed.

Her name was Aida, like the opera, and I said I'd heard it meant happy in Italian. More laughter. *Oh, I always live up to it.* She was aggressive in the pursuit of her pleasure. She claimed a stool at the counter and insisted I serve right there. Her father was detained on business. When I suggested that I hold the meal for an hour or two, show her to her seat in one of the lavish dining rooms, she shrugged. *What's the point? The man has no taste. That's why he sent me to evaluate.*

She was unsettling, rapacious. Could go from languid to kinetic, every movement sparking. Her upper lip was full and a smidge too short, her mouth unnervingly parted as if to speak (which she did a lot of) or eat (of which she did even more). She shoved pots aside to view my work and snatched plates without asking permission. She ate hunched over, elbows out, rings dragging through sauce as she exhibited the slovenliness of those rich enough not to care. But she ate. Her tines scraped the plate. Her fingers chased the last drops. She cast her eyes heavenward, groaned. Never before or since have I served a diner whose pleasure was so naked. Yet when the eight courses were done after just forty-five minutes, she sat back, picking grease from her nails, and said, *That wasn't very good, was it?*

My back stiffened. Had I been a cat, I might have hissed.

The menu. It's awful. You did what you could, but as I said, my father has no sense of taste. He would eat a pig's asshole if you called it calamari. I think he may have had certain nerves die in his face. It happened to people in America, if I remember. What's that seaside city, that industrial one— Baltimore? Providence? Chemical runoff seeped into the water and just like that—she snapped her fingers—*people woke up unable to taste the thirty-four flavors in dark chocolate.*

Are there thirty-four? I said, dazed by the glut of language.

As many as seventy-eight, if you believe Roland Barthes. Her narrow eyes narrowed further. *Wasn't his cookbook on pâtisserie required reading at Le Cordon Bleu?*

Right. I love Barthes. I'd forgotten my fake education. *So tell me more about yourself,* I said to change the topic.

She stayed for hours, topping off her wine and sharing more than I asked for. She was twenty years old and enrolled at the University of Milan, or had been, before serious doubts as to the air quality in that city. This seemed not to bother her. I couldn't tell what bothered her. The fur slipped off her shoulder and she shrugged it back again and again, so that it was impossible to discern nonchalance from a chill. She loved fast cars, the work of a choreographer named Charlotte Edmonds, and her two new puppies. *Cats I fail to understand.* She did not trust her father's culinary instincts. *So when he suggested I visit the kitchen, I took the lying bastard up on his offer.* A pause, assessing. *You are exactly to his taste.*

Crudeness came sheathed in that genteel accent, the blade so fine it took a beat to feel its deep, sudden bite. I scrubbed a pot as if I hadn't heard.

It's the truth, love, she said condescendingly, as if I didn't have nine years on her. *He lies. How do you think he made his fortune?* She walked me through the basics. Her father had made a windfall buying saline IV drips and reselling them at markup when consecutive pandemics hit. Same with grain reserves and famine, with coal and electricity during a winter of freak blizzards. He had a nose for scarcity and impending disaster. He'd bought the land on this mountain long before the smog.

How long?

Aida took a slow sip, savoring the drama. *Nearly a decade ago.*

Impossible.

She grinned with bits of pistachio in her teeth. Back when the mountain held little value for the Italian government, her father had purchased it thinking to withdraw from a public that hated him for his success. The real timeline of events had been obscured for fear of general outcry. *They already called him*—she smirked—*a prophet of doom. Imagine the rattle of those tiny, superstitious brains if they knew how long agricultural experiments have been part of our contingency plan. People are jealous. They lack foresight.* Acceding to the recent demand for sunlight, her father had ramped up preexisting research and made a deal to share findings with the government. He'd even begun leasing land to investors who brought private funding to the venture, along with complementary values of self-sufficiency, innovation, isolation, et cetera. But rather than express gratitude, her father's lessees hated him too. They were oil tycoons and tech titans and heiresses from Italy and Europe and sometimes the Americas, and they had never experienced what it was to be beholden. They despised her father for dangling the key to their fates. It didn't help that he so infrequently mingled, that he was prone to pedantry, that he came from a different social milieu. *They know he doesn't belong.* Hence the restaurant. The Sunday dinners held here were meant to have a civilizing effect. The plan was to wine and dine the most valuable investors into obeisance. Aida spoke as if of pigs or cattle. *Stick some Xanax in the trough to keep them happy. Kidding, of course.* Was she? On the topic of her father she was scathing. *I've told him to forget those snobs. He's thirsty for their adulation.* She returned to the topic of her father and the residents like a person unable to stop scratching an infected bite until, desperate for reprieve, I asked about her mother.

Gone. Aida pulverized another pistachio.

I'msorryforyourloss, I said. The conversation slipped, suddenly icy, and I sought a foothold. *Your mother, what was she?* I hadn't seen another person in so long. I was hungry for a connection I saw in Aida's cheekbones, her tidy nose. *Japanese, or Taiwanese, or—*

Is. Not was. I saw her father in her then. His broad shoulders on her narrow frame, his cold black eyes. *I didn't say dead. She abandoned us. Don't ask, it's too dull.*

How—

She flared then, incendiary in red fur. *Did I stutter? Who the fuck are you to pry? I know you didn't attend Le Cordon Bleu or run the kitchen at Coloniál. Count yourself lucky that my father still wanted you after the background check. I suppose your photo helped.* That stung, but not so much as what she said next. *You're just some mediocre cook and this is* our *country, and I say you are not to ask about my mother.*

The casual meal had fooled me, Aida's legs swinging from the stool had fooled me. That soft mouth of hers had fooled me, as had the laughter it released, so unmannered that I thought of it as innocent, a child's. I remembered that my job—my true job—was to please. I apologized.

In magnanimous tones, Aida proclaimed that I should have her help with future menus. Her good mood returned as we discussed plans for the next dinner party, the real one, six guests in two Sundays. By the time she left, we'd hammered out a schedule. Aida would return to help taste. She oinked as she passed through the door. *Let's win the love of the pigs. Oh, and they don't read Barthes at Le Cordon Bleu. You should, though. Not for his thoughts on chocolate, but on wine and language.*

He emerged as I was dumping the dregs of Aida's wine. *Coward*, I groused as the cat flowed onto the counter. He gagged on a crumb of pâté. I took up the phone. As stipulated in my contract, the landline was to be used in case of emergency.

My employer picked up on the second ring. *Yes?*

It was my first time hearing his voice, or so I thought. His English was British too, hyperarticulated to the point of sounding like a GPS. Hairs rose at the back of my neck. But I couldn't sit in agony, wondering if I'd find myself stripped of my visa and thrown off-mountain. I said, *Do you intend to fire me?*

No.

I waited; nothing more came. An altitude headache throbbed behind my left eye. *But you know I lied on my application.*

He must have put a hand over the receiver. Sounds muffled, a door slammed, and then he said, into absolute silence, *I offered a salary commensurate to your experience, forty percent less than if your résumé had been truthful. You came cheap. Your—stories—indicate a certain flexibility that is valuable to me. You have other skills I may draw upon.*

I did not bring up my application photo. *I'm willing to take on whatever I need for this role. If there's a class for me to learn Italian, or books—*

Not necessary. The great privilege of your position is that you may cook protected from the world's distractions. Is that not what you want?

Yes. I said it again: *Yes.*

Good. You are reasonably adept in the kitchen, as my daughter has reported.

Aida had left perhaps twenty minutes earlier. This was my first inkling of how close the bridge between father and daughter, how swift and strong the current that ran beneath. I didn't think anything of it that night. I was distracted by another shiny lure. Vanity made me say, *What other skills do I have?*

"I will faithfully perform any task within reason, and with dignity."

My own words, read back, were mocking. I almost hung up to preserve what little dignity I retained. Then I thought, why the hell not. *What's your wife's name?*

The pause was so long I thought we'd been disconnected. *Eun-Young*, he said, and hung up.

Three

❧

And that is how, in the depths of that surreal country in a
flavorless world, I discovered, among various fruits, vegetables, and animals believed extinct, the last specimen of my
professional pride. Shriveled, squashed—but extant.

It helped that I dreamed of my employer. Brief dreams, long dreams,
foggy dreams, dreams so clear that I saw each string of spit form in his
mouth as he said, *Cheap*. Sometimes Aida's voice piped in, wry, com-
manding: *Mediocre*. This wasn't lust, despite the nights I dreamt my
employer tall and handsome, squat and troll-like, blond, hunchbacked,
spectral, naked but for one black eye. Each dream traveled inexorably
toward the moment at which he cast my food off the mountain. I woke
up with my jaw clenched. Cooked with something to prove.

Aida swung by with cookbooks, dietary stipulations, menus. To
nouvelle and classique French fare we added Neolithic recipes free of
dairy, medieval Italian recipes heavy on squash and almonds, early
agrarian recipes so crammed with husky, fibrous grains that they would,
in Aida's words, *Make you shit till you see god*. Modern additions included
a vegan diet beloved of the world's best cricket player, astronaut supple-
ments for bone density, foods charcoal-infused and nitrate-free. Never

anything from her mother's side, nothing Korean. *What a cliché*, Aida said, rolling her eyes when I suggested she might miss kimchi. *My mother didn't care about food.*

Same, I said.

Then you should know better. She crossed cabbage off the menu. *It's not that easy to go home again.*

My employer demanded that we spare no effort in testing toward recipes that were, in his words, optimal. To him this meant a reach back through time and tradition, at great expense. My god, the wasted wagyu and caviar and saffron. *You can't deny the nutritional superiority of time-tested ingredients*, Aida snapped, and then, *Okay, yeah, classic nouveau riche behavior.*

I eyed her, uncertain as to her ability to mock herself—but then she grinned. The space between us eased.

Our pièce de résistance was a traditional preparation of poularde de Bresse en vessie: an entire chicken, stuffed with truffles and foie, steamed inside an inflated pig's bladder in a bath of liquor and still more truffles. The ingredients were all Vegas, the presentation of the bird in its smooth gray sac austere, even foreboding, a dish I imagined serving to prima ballerinas if ballerinas could eat. Things came to a head when I argued that we should steam the poultry in water for our trial runs—I balked at pouring gallons of Madeira and rare Armagnac down the drain. I can't say why I drew that line, on that day. From this distance I can hardly see the lines, which were so blurred, so constantly shifting.

Aida fired back when I concluded a half-assed defense of artisans, respect, so forth. *Why fixate on the alcohol? The chicken is genuine Bresse.*

Bresse, that vintage French breed, white-feathered and blue-legged, more costly to raise than any other—and slaughtered to the last bird when chicken feed was diverted to avert human starvation. I managed to keep from saying that this, too, was impossible. *I thought we were leaving the Bresse name on the menu as, as a tribute.*

You don't know my father. He insisted on the real thing once he heard it described as the poultry of kings. Aida rattled off figures. The bribe to the French minister of health. The smuggler's fee. The payment to a hundred-odd Lyonnais farming families for the exclusive right to the breed and the name, into perpetuity. *Bresse is now a misnomer. The birds should have our name. Imagine them choking on* that. *Still, I agree we can omit the Madeira and Armagnac until the real meal.* She leaned in, conspiratorial. *What's the fun without a bit of risk?*

She wasn't cruel, Aida. At her best, as I came to know her, she was curious and exacting and driven. Under her gaze I stuffed and blended and cured and piped and batonnéted, fielding questions about what temperatures I aimed for, why I blanched before I fried, chose parsley over cilantro. *Too harsh*, I explained. *The root of cilantro is the Greek word for bedbug.*

That got a smile out of her. I was learning what else did. For all that her references were global, her outfits avant-garde, Aida, like her father, was a bit of a culinary traditionalist. Slide a classic terrine beneath her nose, tease her with textbook soufflé whipped from butter so rich it blushed orange—she'd smile, or let out a string of curses, or, best yet, go silent as she slid a spoon into that quiver. (*Go light, light, light.*) She'd close her eyes. She'd part her lips and moan.

I thought of my pastry chef, and not just because strawberries glowed brazen in the greenhouse, not because when I lay my used, aching body down each night it echoed the ache of sex. I remembered his lessons after lust was sated and pride set aside to cool. With his breath that smelled of flour, he'd say—what was it? Something about feeding a person other than yourself. Something about inspiration. *A little more*, Aida might begin, and I knew, before she finished, to reach for lemon, or salt. As I had no appetite of my own, I guided my cooking by hers.

Late into the nights I confited and minced and pressed and clarified, making up, by dint of technical precision, for the palate I could no longer trust. I cut my thumb, pulled a muscle, and one day I burned my left forearm in a mirror of a burn on my right. I had the dizzy sensation of being overlaid on my life from seven years earlier, and I clung to that feeling of being twenty-two and ambitious. For all that came after, I remain grateful for that. I will always be grateful for that. My employer gave me a job; he gave me a reason to live.

But I was no longer the person I'd been at twenty-two. In preparing for that dinner I cooked for Aida, for my employer, for imagined guests, for my pride, for the numbers ticking up in my bank account and down in the ledger of my debt, for the right to breathe clean air, feel the lick of sun, live in that country. But at twenty-nine I could no longer stomach my food: I didn't cook for myself. Once I had. Once upon a time I'd left Los Angeles and been swallowed down the throat of a life in which my sole loyalty was to my tongue. My belly. Myself. My mother called me selfish and so selfish I became. From nineteen to twenty-five I was a mouth, sating. For myself I made three-day braises and chose the most marbled meats, I played loose with butter and cream. My arteries were young, my life pooling before me, and I lapped, luxurious, from it. I drank, smoked, flew cheap red-eyes around Europe, I lived in thrilling shitholes, I found pills that made nights pass in a blink or expanded time to a soap bubble, floating, luminous, warm. Time seemed infinite, then. I begged famous chefs for the chance to learn from them. I entered competitions and placed in a few. I volunteered to work brunch, turn artichokes, clean the grease trap. I flung my body at all of it: the smoke and singe of the grill station, a duck's breast split open like a geode, two hundred oysters shucked in the walk-in, sex in the walk-in, drunken rides around Paris on a rickety motorcycle and no helmet, a white truffle I stole and shaved in secret over a bowl of Kraft mac 'n' cheese for me, just me, as my body strummed the high taut selfish song of youth. On my twenty-fifth birthday I served black-market fugu to my guests, the neurotoxin stinging sweetly on my lips as I waited to see if I would, by eating, die. At that age I believed I knew what death was: a thrill, like brushing by a friend who might become a lover.

And then came the day—I was already a little weary, my stomach a little heavy—when I left the pin bones in an appetizer of fried young sardines. I liked the crunch, and so I left them in. Deboned, said the menu, and I left them in. The chef was out that day. An old woman was the first customer at 11:34 in the morning, a woman with so thick a string of pearls around her neck, so strangling a string, that I thought it was her jewelry that choked her. Now I must be older than she was. That day her mortality yawned open like a door through which I glimpsed my mother, who had died the week before. The customer survived; no matter. I was fired. I lost my nerve. When I looked for work again, months later, the smog had begun its spread. The American border shut me out. These are but a few points in a global story of catastrophe that I'm not narcissistic enough to claim for my own—and yet. In that old woman's face I glimpsed the aging face of the mother I hadn't seen in years: a stranger choked by my food. I lost the desire to cook. I'd previously cursed my ambition, which left me discontent, penniless, envious, forever eyeing others' fuller plates, but to be without was far worse. Agony, gray days without appetite, occasional pills that turned less occasional, a flirtation with a high bridge from which I was saved by the appearance of two tourists asking that I take their photo, lost friends, lost paychecks, a promise to myself to stay alive if only to see Los Angeles again, night and the death of the stars.

Like every cook, I blamed the smog. In truth, it was more than that. A universe within me had already been flickering out. By the time I set foot on that mountain I felt myself to be a void, a null space, a set of hands for hire.

But I could still give a damn good dinner party.

Aida arrived at dawn in an electric-blue G-Wagon outfitted with custom exhausts. *Open it*, she commanded as she thrust forward a greasy bag. A parrot's worth of plumage swung from her ears. Two burritos plumped into my hand as she said, shyly, from behind lime-green glasses, *I thought you might miss California.*

No—she wasn't cruel.

The burritos oozed cannellini beans in rich, green oil. I claimed I'd had my breakfast while Aida tore in. *I drove to Milan for this because I heard promising rumors—but it's cheap industrial wheat.* She stuck out a tongue so clean and velvet, I felt the inexplicable urge to stroke it. *Still, this is fuel.* I was surprised when she gestured for my burrito, too. Primly, pushing her glasses up like an old woman, she said, *Well, I went all that way. We can't waste it.*

My breath caught. I took an obedient nibble. Before the oil gagged me, I felt a brief flash of appetite, reflected off hers.

Aida raced through preparations. Hand-lettered place cards, personal notes to each guest that referenced their hobbies and flattered their vanities. Two hundred candles went up in the most intimate dining room. *The mood should be soft. Persuasive.* Bowls of candied fennel seeds beloved of one guest, an Iranian meteorologist. Thick, lavender-scented towels in the bathroom on which the bulimic Italian actress could wipe her spindly hands before returning to the table. Enormous hothouse roses named in honor of a famous ruby belonging to the South African couple whose family fortune had been exhumed, two centuries earlier, from out of that continent's first mine. Aida let slip that her father was courting the couple for their diamonds—not to wear, but to replace parts in machinery. *There's always something to optimize.*

Aida herself was the final touch, iridescent in snakeskin, eyelids dotted gold. Her hair rose in crazy geometries. *You look*—I considered her—*out of this world. Is there a dress code I should know about?*

Oh, she said, and *Shit,* and *I thought he told you.* There was a speck of parsley in her teeth. I watched it bob as she explained that, per her father's orders, per my contract, I was to remain out of sight during dinners. *Belowground,* she stressed. *And I almost forgot, my father wants this added to the dessert course. He said to use the pits, too.*

For all her jokes about pills and pigs, there was nothing pharmaceutical in the wrinkled, thumb-sized dates Aida gave me. I bit into one. As I didn't collapse, or foam at the mouth, I blitzed both fruit and pit into a powder that I folded through batter, the surface glossing rusty, red.

The salad went up, I went down. Aida had instructions for reheating and serving the dishes.

Best seat in the house, I said to the cat, who blinked, irate at my invasion of his security closet. On the live feed I saw guests arrive at the door. Their grainy forms did not resemble the petty ghouls Aida had described. They looked well-kept, at ease, unremarkable apart from the South African woman's obscene string of diamonds.

I scanned the limited DVD selection: either Korean dramas or classic Italian films. Curiously, the latter hailed from the silent era, voiceless. There were a few English novels (too long), a collection of poems (too emotional). I passed over the travel-sized Italian-English dictionary I'd brought in my luggage, now stashed behind a vase; after my employer's reaction to the idea of Italian lessons, I suspected the book would be seen as contraband. In the end I read, and regretted, a short story about Bengali immigrants in twentieth-century America. I knew the cities named, yet the story's underpinning optimism was unrecognizable, disquieting, like coming home to a house suddenly built on sand. *As ordinary as it all appears*, the last line read, *there are times when it is beyond my imagination.* In the end I entertained myself with past glories. *You know*, I told the cat, *I once had a diner clap for me.* He was alert, swishing his tail to the scents that blew through the vent.

I detected the veal as it left the oven. I winced when Aida overtorched the candied carrots. And I knew the precise moment she cut open the poularde de Bresse en vessie. Out rolled the great fragrant mist of Armagnac and Madeira, a heady golden carpet that invited me back to Paris. I closed my eyes to the basement. I went.

Imagine:

It is five years earlier, the year of my triumph. I've been chosen to stage at Coloniál, the Michelin-starred restaurant that I will one day lie about running. Stage is restaurant-speak for *free labor*, but I'm unconcerned. One day I expect to be sous chef there, if not executive chef, if not there then somewhere better. I'm twenty-four. There is no smog. I'm so impatient for my life to begin that I've flown to Paris a month early and taken a catering job to pass the time. A politician is holding an engagement feast for his daughter, thirty-two courses and twenty guests. It is one of the last of its kind, though none of us know it. All we know is that the banquet is to be kept secret from the public (in the countryside, on the streets, across certain internet forums if you know to listen, whispers about supply chains, crop blights kept under wraps in America, the prices of milk and beef). A van rattles us out of Paris, past herds of woolly sheep, the green-slatted light of buckwheat in the fields. (That wheat will be extinct in three years, the sheep piled in bloody mounds within two.) But for now: wildflowers, a farmhouse kitchen, herbs in great fragrant boughs, and twenty ortolans drowned in Armagnac. The dining room falls silent when the rare songbirds are served, whole. In the kitchen we turn off the radio and listen for the crunch of bones.

I was a chef in Paris, I said to the cat, who looked at me, and sighed, and didn't ask if the tears I shed into his fur were for the dead birds, or the fact that I would never taste one, or the prick of old ambition. Not until that moment did I know I yearned to be in the spotlight, watching guests exclaim, watching Aida eat with relish.

Self-pity ended at a deafening crash from above.

More crashing followed. A man bellowed, indistinct. I climbed closer to the vent as other voices wove in. Feet thudded along the hall, toward the front door, and soon the Iranian meteorologist appeared in miniature on the security feed, his body a study in fury.

My employer followed. I saw a slice of his pixelated face as he leaned into the meteorologist's ear; I saw anger go out of the meteorologist until he reached, like dough, the pliable stage for shaping. The men went back inside. I smelled coffee. An hour later Aida came down, the feathers in her ears making the cat peer up in interest.

Brilliant. I haven't seen my father this happy since god knows when. She undid her earrings, unclasped her boots. A fug of sweat and heat came off her legs, strong but not unpleasant, reminiscent of locker rooms, slumber parties, other relics. Though it was hot, she kept her socks on. *They're perfectly docile now. An absolute triumph. The South Africans and the Iranian have agreed to contribute to infrastructure improvements.*

How were the dates?

Beyond compare. She turned her attention to the Korean rom-com playing on the antiquated TV. There were no English subtitles, and as best as I could make out, the wealthy main character had ended up living among poor villagers, in disguise. It struck me that she was my opposite. *Oh, I love* Crash Landing on You. *Wait till the hot rival shows up.*

You know Korean?

Mostly insults. Jugeullae? She snapped her teeth. *It means, do you want to die?*

Not especially. What I want— I tapped at my incisor and watched Aida try to pick the parsley from her own. At last, impatient, I stepped in with a dishtowel and wiped her teeth.

I flushed as soon as I'd done it. *Sorry. Childhood habit.*

She pressed her fingers to her mouth. Turned back to the screen. We watched the rest of the episode.

That they were just dates was true, from a biological and ecological perspective. Hardy plants of the desert, *Phoenix dactylifera* still clung to high-elevation zones of Central Asia and North Africa. Dried stores were fairly copious. The dates served at dinner were common enough, except that they had come from the branches of one specific date palm on one family compound in Iran, a compound that had stood for six generations before it was reduced to rubble by an errant American drone strike.

My employer fed the meteorologist dates from the last crop produced by his family tree, and broke this news only after the guests had chewed and swallowed the dessert course, after they had moved to apéritifs, after the fruit was partially digested, irretrievable from its bath of stomach acids. The Iranian scientist, upon learning this, jammed two fingers down his own throat with a swiftness that must have awoken the actress's admiration. He recovered nothing beyond a few papery fragments of skin. The crash was the sound of him sweeping dishes from the table with his soiled hand.

Only at the threshold of the restaurant, out of sight of other diners, did my employer tell the meteorologist that not all the dates had been consumed. Several dozen remained hidden in the mountain's research facilities, in perfect condition for planting. Just as protected, just as much in my employer's power, was the meteorologist's young cousin, who had been out of the house when the drone struck. The seeds were viable, my employer promised. Many futures remained. It was those possibilities I saw working the malleable dough of the meteorologist's face as he stood on the steps of the restaurant that night.

As a young prodigy, the meteorologist had headed a team that cleared skies above Olympic ceremonies. He was the world's leading expert in the field of cloud seeding. My employer wanted the best of the best, and so found the right price at which to lure the meteorologist from his tenure at a public university. This story I heard much later, from my employer, when we'd become closer than I thought possible. What remains unclear is how much Aida knew.

The truth of Aida, I think, lay not in these schemes, however faithfully she played her role to the bitter end. She sat and she chattered and she ate—and yet. I was shaken awake that same night, the Korean drama still casting blues and oranges on the wall. *Come quick or we'll miss it*, Aida said. Her face was scrubbed of makeup, a zit forming on her chin. We emerged from beneath the marble tongue. It was just eleven o'clock. The empty restaurant seemed bigger, darker, more full of doors. She passed without asking through my bedroom's EMPLOYEES ONLY door. *I promised you a surprise*, she said as she pushed the bathroom mirror and entered the space beyond.

The glass eye of that hidden room stared out into total darkness. The drop sang out below. Aida ignored the tight quarters as, on her knees, she unzipped the waiting briefcase and began to assemble its contents into a telescope. Minutes later she let out a sigh so replete that I startled, looking around for a torrone, a terrine, the only things I knew of, at the time, that could produce in her such a sound of satisfaction. But she was looking at the sky.

She guided me into position. Through the lens I saw a black circle, the frill of my own lashes, and then two bright discs that slid by one another. No—there was a place at the edge where they overlapped. That edge blazed with alien colors. *The conjunction of Jupiter and Saturn. I was thinking about this all night, every time that bitch told another putrid story about her diamonds.* It hadn't occurred to me that Aida was anything but content at the table. As I'd yearned to be upstairs, she'd cast her thoughts even higher.

I prefer this room, she said after we'd looked our fill. *Though the telescope at my father's house is more powerful. This space was a mistake on the builders' part, a flaw in the glass they tried to hide. I insisted they keep it because when you lie down, it feels like—well, I'll show you.*

We lay down, a tight fit. Aida looked out. I did the same. A few stars, sure, a ridge of mountain, but not so different from the view in other rooms. My leg cramped. I shifted as quietly as I could.

What feeling? I said when I began to lose sensation from contact with the freezing glass.

Not this, Aida exploded. She sat up. Fisted hands in her hair. *There's something wrong, let me think, let me think—of course! Fucking idiot I am.* She stepped over me, and for a moment seemed unnervingly tall, a different species. She shut off the bathroom lights. *Wait*, she said as she returned. *Our eyes will adjust.*

Without those lights it grew colder than ever, and darker. Our reflections disappeared. The glass disappeared. After a time, my body disappeared. It was the strangest feeling to have no point of fixation amongst that drowning darkness, to lose, as minutes ticked by, any sense of proportion. My body disappeared, or rather it changed. It became a kernel of cold, a pinprick folded within the rippling hugeness of me; or the cold had become its own enormous, stately ship, and I rode its bleak surface. An embryonic state. I floated, and Aida began to speak. As a girl she'd run away from home. They lived in a house abutting a hill that shimmered with olive trees. The walk from the back door to the edge of the trees was less than thirty minutes. She took snacks and water, set out right after breakfast in her new swimsuit. She intended to sunbathe long enough to make her mother worry, then return for lunch. Beneath the shadow of the first olive, she encountered a sudden desire to be home, and so turned around. Straight there and back in the tidy, constant sunshine. When she walked through the door, her mother slapped her. She had been missing for six hours. Straight there and back: six hours. Her snacks and water were untouched, her bikini secure in its rabbit-ears knot. Later, she timed the walk. Twenty-two minutes. Forty if she slowed as much as she was able. There was never any accounting for that lost time. Aida's voice lapped me like fluid as she said that was the day she glimpsed the clear, thin membrane that separated her from this world. I don't know how long her telling took. Over the years, certain details have become vague to me—did she say the olive trees shimmered, or did she say they waved? Was the water cold? Did her mother burn or shred the swimsuit?—but even that is evasion; in truth, those details became vague mere seconds after I heard them, as do the edges of dream. Suspended that night in glass, wrapped in the arrow of Aida's story, I felt us traveling together at great speed toward the cusp of some place, perhaps the same place time had gone when Aida was small. *That day I knew*, she said. *Neither my father nor I are like anyone else. There's no place for us here.* I must have slept at some point, a sleep such as I have not had since, a swift and speeding passage yet weightless, frictionless, a sleep that took me far and brought me back fresh and unaching to a sound that echoed in the still-dark night. It was a cry that seemed to come from the planets themselves. It was ancient and very new. It is a sound I can only describe as red.

Aida was sitting up, smiling. *My dogs. They're old enough to sing.*

Come morning, I dragged the remains of dinner to the cliff. As the black bags plummeted into the dump I mostly managed to avoid thoughts of starving children in Saigon and Syria and Middle America. There was one bad moment when a bag snagged on a protrusion and folded like a person bent at the waist—but then it exploded in béarnaise and truffle oil.

Either Jupiter or Saturn was still visible, pale against the lightening sky. The wind was blustery and full of voices. I sat as sun lipped the horizon. The grass changed in the light, from brown to yellowish to green. The grass: it was green.

It was the end of March. I'd been in the country for three weeks. All around me, as if the scales had fallen from my eyes, I saw color flushing the slopes, a color I'd never again hoped to see: that green that is the herald of flavor and pleasure, that says: *look*, says: *wait*, says: *taste*: the gates of the underworld unlatched for mints and sorrels and pine-dark needles in shade and the pale sun-swell of the honeysuckle that bells out the triumphant return, after long winter, of a daughter. It was a green made possible by a man who held in his sway horticulturalists and biologists and chicken geneticists and meteorologists who could control the weather itself, and I forgot those wan, distant orbs in the sky as I opened my mouth, I bayed.

And then, at last, it was spring.

Four

❦

In May I began crying upwards of five times a day. I say crying but it seemed untethered from any emotion, involuntary, like clear snot from the eyes. At first I blamed allergies (the grass grew pinprick flowers), and then I blamed the peppers in my employer's new recipes (meant to stimulate the metabolism), and then I blamed the K-dramas (four more, each sappier, each more affecting for the fact that I didn't comprehend a word). In the end, I suspected the cleanliness of my new life. I was a few weeks from the end of my trial period, and there was no way I'd get the permanent position if I admitted my need for menthols to wake up in the mornings, weed to zombify me into sleep, a few grams of coke or MDMA now and again to feel alive. Not with my employer's rules and Aida's twelve-step skincare routines. When my illegal stash ran out, I had no choice but to keep my mind terrifyingly clear through all the ticked hours of the day. Crying was a side effect, a brutal detox.

My god do your eyes look tiny, Aida said as she pushed through the door.

Good morning to you, too.

I'm telling you because I care. In her compact mirror, my eyes were dull nails in the gaunt shelf of my face. *It's not racist because I'm half Asian. Eat more collagen. You know, I never see you eat. Vitamin D helps, too. Sunshine. Why are you holed up in here? Come with me when I walk the dogs.*

My job is here. I couldn't bear to ask if she knew I needed permission to leave.

A doctor called the landline the next day. On his orders, using a sterile package of supplies left for me in the storeroom, I took my blood pressure, my temperature, my pulse, my weight. He asked about my sleeping habits and the frequency of my dreams, when I'd last drunk and the patterns of my urination. He agreed about walks and vitamin D. *And you could stand to gain a few kilos. Otherwise, you're quite healthy for someone of your generation.* It wasn't until hanging up that I realized: amidst the bodily trivia, he had not asked for my name.

Mine was the first generation predicted to live more briefly than each of the previous three. Generation Mayfly, went the joke, and I was, in fact, born in May. The day the World Health Organization released its report on life expectancy, I was working at a family-run inn in Basque Country. They were a dramatic ensemble, that family, three generations of barbacks, line cooks, and servers who bumped elbows in a drafty farmhouse, gossiping and kissing one another's cheeks and shit-talking in ever-shifting alliances. To call service bad on the day of the report is an understatement. The bartender launched himself in an explosion of glassware at his father, the front-of-house manager, with accusations of BPA-filled baby bottles, cigars smoked over the crib, et cetera. The rest of the family soon turned on itself, nephews against uncles, grandchildren against beloved mamie. It was sordid, incredible. The afternoon diners watched in delight. Two chairs were broken, an inheritance refused, then reinstated. And me? Not my family. I acted as referee. I pried the bartender's hands from his father's neck. Stroked the junior waiter's curls and explained that his mother, the hostess, had done what she thought best when she took him each summer to swim in a lightly carcinogenic lake. *La moitié de ta vie est finie*, he sobbed. He was saying that half my life was over. I didn't care to get into details, just handed him a napkin.

I was already used to it, I might have said, the way I was used to emergency weather warnings, to pain from a wrist broken and badly reset. I'd been hearing that my life would amount to little since I decided to enter the kitchen at nineteen.

I was a disappointment to my mother, an extension of her body gone haywire, much like the valve in her heart that would fatally betray her. She was born to poverty in rural China and managed—the only one in her village—to win a scholarship to study medicine in Beijing. Then she won a coveted visa to America. Then she met a handsome Korean American entrepreneur. It was supposed to go onwards and upwards from there, but the engine sputtered, the song died out. My father turned out to be a wife-beating shithead who walked out, her Chinese medical credentials were worth less than the cheap toilet paper with which she wiped the asses of the elderly in her new job as nursing home aide, we lived in run-down apartments shared with families of silverfish. If this gives my mother the gleam of some tragic college-essay immigrant heroine, rest assured she did not see herself that way. Throughout my childhood she maintained an ironclad optimism neither feigned nor destructible, unashamed to ask relatives for money orders and the Mexican grocery for a deal on bruised fruit. So focused was her gaze that she moved blinkered to jeers and pity both, befriending through dumb attrition even the winos who asked her how much, how much did she cost. She proudly referred to herself as a welfare queen, misunderstanding the connotations. She was in America, she explained, regal. In America, her daughter had every opportunity. Her sole and crowning glories were me, and the apartment she purchased with her life's savings the summer after my high school graduation.

I remember the door, freshly painted, and the scrape of my mother's key in the lock. I remember the neighborhood she chose, shabby but out of Pasaje: Los Angeles at long last. The apartment was a short hop from UCLA, where I'd just gotten in off the waitlist. My envy of graduation gifts that I'd seen my friends collect—meals, vacations, cars—dissolved in the stink of turpentine as I understood that the apartment was meant for me. For us. My mother showed off living room, bedroom, washer-dryer combo. *You can drop off clothes, save your time to study.* I left before lunch, begging a headache due to paint fumes. But as soon as I walked past the nearest taqueria, as I felt the grease settle on my skin, and heard the scrape of spatulas on the grill, as soon as I ordered and felt the immensity of my relief—I think I knew.

I squandered every opportunity my mother had earned by dropping out before sophomore year. There ended the chance for me—for us— to be a real American doctor. *A cook?* my mother said when I came to deliver the news. *You will be a kind of servant.*

And I said—we were the same person, after all—*You mean like you are?*

I pushed into her kitchen with my shopping bags. What was the color of those walls? I was looking at my hands. They destemmed herbs from the fancy market. They skinned cleaned trimmed fish into filets of radiant geometry. My hands—shoulders—wrists—ribs—spine—gave into the rhythm of the kitchen that pounds, insistent, drowning out past and future and duplicitous whispering mind, an exultant demand for now now *now* broken when my mother said, *Is that all?*

She looked up from the plate I'd set before her. No clink of knife or fork. Into that deathly silence, she said, *Where are the bones. The head.* Rising, pushing up her sleeves, she went to the dirty sink. Up in her fist came skin, scales, tail, roughage, discards.

She was still at the sink by the time I finished packing. The plate I'd made for her was still pristine, but colder. *Selfish*, I heard her say. *Who are you?* Only the cat would meet my gaze as I walked out, and so I took him as a dare.

My mother didn't turn.

That was the last time I saw her. We disagreed on food, fundamentally. My mother was an awful cook, a point of obscure pride retained from her impoverished childhood. Sustenance mattered over taste. She saved the water from soaked beans. She stewed the flesh of November's discount Halloween pumpkins. The consolation of night shift was, for her, the thrill of bearing home, in each fresh dawn, the just-expired boxes of Kraft and Hamburger Helper, the Jell-O cups filmed over beneath their lids. *Cold drinks will give you stomach cancer*, she said when she refused me sodas from the concession stand. The T-bone she bought for my birthday she cooked to rubber, boiling the bone not once but twice till the resulting broth ran clear. *No waste this way. Raw meat will kill you. French food is not made for us, too heavy, it will kill you.* Eating dairy despite my mild lactose intolerance would kill me; throwing my future away would kill me; my lack of respect for thrift, severity, real work would kill me. Her predictions became transitive. We were one body, after all. *You will kill me*, my mother said, grimly. And at other times: *I will kill you.*

Jugeullae?

I fixed myself a meal, just what the doctor ordered. Chicory under crisp lardons. Whole-wheat heritage-grain bread. A filet of mackerel that shimmered with omega-3s. But after a few bites the lardons went greasy on my tongue, the fish a wash of rancid sea. I threw my plate to the ground.

The cat sniffed around the shards. His fur had grown matted, as if, along with appetite, he'd lost the urge to groom. How unkempt a creature, how ill-suited to our elegant surrounds. I knew, and hated, the image we made: a pair of starvelings.

My appetite would acclimate, I told myself, just as my eyes had gotten used to the light. It must.

I shooed the cat into the storeroom before Aida arrived. Standing in that spotless kitchen, I informed her of my interest in a walk. I'd have to plan out my tasks, check my schedule with—

I already spoke with my father, she interrupted. *He thinks it's a great idea.*

I pretended this was a normal exchange.

Aida roared up the drive in a bone-white racing car and matching leather jacket. In the backseat sat two slips of flame with long, thin snouts. *From an ancient Egyptian line*, she said. The dogs accepted my caresses politely, but their red faces tracked her. *Sini and Des are practically an extension of me. I've trained them since their whelping.*

Odd, she said, observing us. *They don't typically take to strangers.*

The dogs were licking my jacket. I didn't mention that this was where the cat had slept, and that we might be seeing the demonstration of a different desire. *How long have you been breeding dogs?*

Eight years.

As she spoke of her forty-year plan to craft the perfect hound, and three hundred other breeding programs in the mountain's labs, Aida revealed a grip of genetics that was firm yet nonchalant, cloaking a muscular intelligence as her posh accent cloaked her crudeness. This was the moment I began to suspect the depth of the endeavor in the land of milk and honey, my glimpse into the heart of a girl I'd thought cool and disdainful. Her words sloshed together in her hurry to get them out. Her eyes went wide. She pressed the gas pedal as she rattled through technical terminology, and soon she'd left my high school knowledge of Punnett squares and brown versus blue eyes in the dust.

You don't have to look so shocked. I'm not an idiot just because I'm young and pretty, she said, tartly, when I was silent.

To be honest, I found it hard to speak. Aida had rolled down every window and the wind slapped my eyeballs. My nose ran, my breath came shallow, my fingers were cold pebbles jammed against my palms. I couldn't remember being so uncomfortable; I couldn't remember being so alive. It had rained the night before. We crashed through huge brown puddles. I had no idea why she insisted on that pristine white car, that speed—except that I do, I did. Suddenly, on that day, I did. Water spangled the arid walls of my soul and I laughed.

Her face went hard. *What's so funny.*

It's not funny! I gasped. *I think I'm—happy. To be honest, I'm too*

dumb to follow along. I didn't finish my own bachelor's, let alone study—
what, exactly, do you study?

Evolutionary biology. With a focus on experimental evolution and gen-
etic drift. More terms: intelligent design, gene editing, backbreeding,
species de-extinction, something called CRISPR that was not a refer-
ence to salad. Aida paused, glanced over, grinned. *But don't let me bore*
you. It isn't my bachelor's, by the way. I was at the University of Milan for
my postdoc.

She must have been no older than ten as an undergraduate. I pictured a scowling miniature in a backpack, Louboutin heels. The Aida
beside me, with something of a child's coyness, promised I would
understand once I saw the labs. We'd stop by to pick up training gear
for the dogs.

We exited the car in a spot like every other: sky, grass, empty field. No
sign of a facility until the earth began to shake. Aida and the dogs stood
like three pieces of statuary as I fell to my knees. *Down, girl*, she said.
Panel after panel of grass slid aside to reveal an elevator the size of a
small house.

Aida shucked, as we descended, her rings, her jacket, her skirt. More
than her thin shins and capable shoulders, more than the freckles spattered down her torso, it was her feet that gave me pause: calloused and
rough, horned as an animal's. She blushed as she stepped into rubber
boots.

I used to dance, she said, pulling jumpsuits from a rack on the wall.

Oh, I said as I shed my own clothes.

The last item was a helmet, vented on both sides and visored with
smoky gray glass. *It's against regulation to take it off*, Aida warned as she

buckled the straps. Out of her heels, she wasn't much taller than me. We faced each other, identical in our uniforms, except for the badge that swung conspicuously from her lanyard. She hung me with an ID card that was plain, white: STAFF. Her hands were at my neck when the elevator doors dinged open.

This was my entry into a world utterly of Aida's creation, and I felt its perfection, its strange seduction. We stood as if within an egg. Vast white dome, curved softly. The ghosts of the storeroom came into life as animals that prowled and dreamed through glass enclosures, radiating out from the center, spoke after reflective spoke, seemingly infinite. Air blew in cool with bleach and musk. Researchers moved across marble floors, and their white coats glowed yellow, red, green; I looked up to a stained-glass window.

Artificial sun, Aida said, but I missed her explanation. I was listening to the music.

Violins wound through the animal cries, horns and cellos too. Absurd, incredible: a piccolo's perfect accompaniment. Tchaikovsky's *Sleeping Beauty* waltz. I still hear it sometimes, from my suburban quiet, its notes rising through the yelp of a neighbor's dog, in the yowl of mating alley cats. I still see Aida walking ahead of me, steps in time to the music.

I see now the line she traced from dance to genetics, arts utterly unlike except that their common medium is time. Down in the labs they froze and reversed it, sped or staccatoed it, and coaxed it to flow one way or another. She herself was changed by its study, able to leap across years so that she shed, down there, her sarcasm and caustic humor, her vestigial childish ways. She strode with purpose into a future that still makes me ache to think of.

The scientists saw what I did. In that skyless domain, they offered not the grudging respect of residents for a landlord, nor the shallow worship of beauty and youth. They looked to Aida as if she were their sun.

Among those who thronged her was a researcher who carried a striking golden chimp. Aida took the animal, which quieted beneath her assessing gaze. She listened to its heart, felt along its limbs, and before relinquishing the chimp she cupped a palm to its furred cheek, a gesture so fleeting no one saw but me.

I hung back, anonymous in my helmet. *I'm not supposed to be here, am I?* I whispered during a lull. *Does your father know—*

She thrust her keycard into my hand. *What are you waiting for? Go on, look.*

There was no end, it seemed, in those heady early days, of doors upon doors upon doors swinging open, the world undressed to bare another luscious fold. A wing of the lab labeled UCCELLI buzzed with the jeweled feathers of hummingbirds and macaws. BESTIAME reeked of countryside: hay and dung, Bresse hens and Berkshire pigs. GATTI was resplendent with leopards and ocelots and a black panther that made me wish I'd brought that morose cat, to provoke and inspire him. After months of confinement to the restaurant, after years of restrictions, to wander was stolen extravagance, like free admission day at the LA Zoo when I'd run from rhino to emu to giraffe, eager to see the sphinxes and dinosaurs. As a child, I'd been told there was a limit to the world. It seemed possible there might be none to Aida's.

I spent longest with Aida's lions. I'd once worked under a terrifying Ukrainian chef who modeled his kitchen after careers in the military and the circus. *You are not the lion,* he bellowed in the face of each young trainee. *You are only the lion feeder.* His food was meticulous, classic, unimpeachable, not unlike what I served in the restaurant on the mountain; but never loose, or free. I watched one of the world's last lions move about its pen like butter slipping around a warm skillet, and tried to inhale its ease.

There were two wings I was unable to interpret. MEGAFAUNA CA-RISMATICA held pandas, penguins, black rhinos, more of those golden chimps. PRELIBATEZZE was home to an armadillo-like creature, further birds, a log rotten with thumb-sized ants.

There you are, Aida said, appearing from the corridor's gloom. I failed to recognize her at first. She had smears of dirt, maybe shit, on her jumpsuit. A stained canvas sack hung over her shoulder. It rustled, briefly.

Like her pups, she panted with eagerness as we drove from the lab. A hundred and forty kilometers per hour, a hundred and sixty, Aida's back never touching the seat. *The de-extinction team has successfully bred a pair of Tasmanian tigers—Tasmanian tigers!* She pounded the wheel and the car swerved. *These will be the first naturally born cubs in a century. The Tasmanian government halted conservation efforts, the cowards.*

Governments have to make hard choices, I said with my eyes on the road. *They'll get to this stuff at some point.*

Choices, Aida said with scorn. We were in descent, the tender green fanned out below. *You mean the way you* chose *to stay in England when America closed its borders?*

I'll get back in. There's a system. A waiting list.

And your place on it?

My face burned. There was nothing to say to that. At a hundred and sixty kilometers per hour we chewed up the road, we ate it. Such movement was, for most, a fantasy. Americans abroad had been given a twenty-four-hour courtesy warning before borders closed; flights booked out in twenty minutes. A protester had time to paint over the Statue of Liberty's GIVE ME YOUR TIRED, YOUR POOR, drawing an eloquent cock and balls before she, despite her green card, was thrown out of the country on a technicality. I thought of my low spot on the reentry list, and the near-impossible conditions of rising higher. Easier to change my skin, my name, become someone else. I reclined my seat, relinquishing knowledge of our speed, giving myself over to the blunt fingers of sun.

I might choose to stay here forever, I said. The world stained warm and red through my shut eyes. *If I could.*

We shouldn't be forced to choose at all. The fury in Aida's voice was familiar. Nostalgic. I'd once possessed that strain of fury, as had my fellow cooks, my friends, my produce guy, a virulent rage against our tainted inheritance of this stupid, smog-choked planet. But it couldn't last. We'd been inoculated from rage by other, more immediate concerns. For example: how to pay rent, how to stay alive. Aida, rich as she was, hadn't been forced to choose between anger and dinner. For the first time in years, I tasted, through her, that feeling.

We descended to the foot of the mountain. Though fences marked the country's perimeter, the true border was the smog that spread perhaps half a mile below. On our side, blue sky capped a vast green field at the mountain's base. The ground was artificially flat. I guessed at future polo fields, a racetrack. *Good idea*, Aida said, and left it at that.

The pups streamed sinuous through chest-high grass. Aida pointed out their large feet and papery ears, drawn from native Italian hounds as well as an extinct wolf of the steppes. *I made sure that there's a place for them out here.*

Just imagine, Aida called as she pushed through the rustling grass. *Imagine we stand here at the end of the Ice Age.* Before smog, before pesticides, before human dominion. A misnomer, she told me. Summers on the continent were long and warm. *Sultry.* Plants grew high to support herds of aurochs and woolly mammoths that numbered in the hundreds of thousands. I soon lost sight of her. The lowering sun sat red and radiant atop the grass. Somewhere, the dogs were running over loam, their feet pattering like fat rain on a summer night. *This biome keeps itself in perfect ecological balance.* Stems stretched higher as Aida's voice passed through, rasping like the fur of one large, contiguous beast. Squinting, I saw mounds. Distant hulkings. *Grazers keep the grasses in check. Ticks and rodents spread disease to cull the genetically inferior, and scavengers dispose of carcasses. There are magnificent apex predators.*

Steppe lions and cave hyenas, Aida said, her disembodied voice adrift with longing. *Bears that stand twelve feet high. I wish the labs could bring them back, but it's been too long. The genetic material has decayed. And so the greatest threat we have today—*

Her voice stopped. I turned in a slow circle. Stalks rattled. A bird gave a low warning call. Out of the greenery burst Aida and her dogs.

Homo sapiens, she said, pinning me. *You. You're the apex predator.*

Her face above me was dappled with grasslight; it flickered between mockery and accusation, between an arrogance I recognized and a raw new fury I felt in the tensing of her wrists, her thighs. My breath caught. *We are the most destructive predators ever seen*, she hissed without a trace of irony. *Me, too. All of us.*

If she expected a fight, I didn't give her one. I lay still, letting her weight push me deeper into the wood-spiced loam. *You sound a little antihuman, Aida.* I took a breath. Earthworms. Rain. Pebbles and copper and salt. *Should I be sleeping with a knife?*

She rolled off, screeching, and came to rest alongside me. *Oh, you're perfectly safe with me. Though you're right, you know. A true commitment to biodiversity requires that we be moderately antihuman.* What did I mean by human, anyhow? *Homo neanderthalensis,* she was quick to remind me, had been close enough kin to crossbreed with *Homo sapiens.* Yet our overhunting had likely led to the older species' destruction. *That is, if we didn't hunt them ourselves.*

This time I saw it—the anger—it wasn't for me. It turned inward. I didn't know how to lift her darkening mood, but the dogs did. Whining and dancing on pointed paws, they licked her until she rose with a fond curse. We resumed our walk.

She seemed lighter after that, less burdened. She pointed out the milk-froth bloom of wild carrots, and nettles spiked with vitamins or good for treating burns. In the folds of the blueing mountains she tracked the ecological footprint of glaciers that had melted eons earlier, leaving alluvial deposits that the country's own agronomists had sown with heirloom grains. *It's our first year planting in this spot, aboveground. We decided it was worth having government inspectors discover the grain and claim its majority. Even the little they leave us will make bread so succulent it brings grown men to their knees. Tasting it, you'll realize you've never had bread before.* I thought I heard in this the same argument her father made through his dietary obsessions: more Neolithic and Paleolithic, more southern French and northern Italian recipes before the influx of foreign spices, before industrial farms and global shipping chains.

I wish my father agreed with me on this topic. What he wants—Here. Tell me what this smells like. She held a tuft of grass to my nose.

Honey, I said, surprised.

Now taste it.

Aida smirked as I spat. The foul flavor came from antioxidants her team had bred into the grass, so that it would be capable of sustaining animals through starvation in a pinch. The idea was adopted from reindeer moss in Siberia. Aida spread her arms. Every blade, every bush, every flower was a living laboratory engineered to feed someone or something, to take toxins out or put nitrogen back in, a piece of an intricate ecological puzzle. *At least that's* my *goal.* She led research, but her father controlled the business side. His investments powered her labs, which meant occasional concessions like this grass.

It shouldn't be here. This sedge grass is decorative bullshit he imported from Northern Asia. The lab spent two years modifying it to slot into our ecosystem, all so that the mountain would literally smell of honey. Terra di latte e miele, she said, mockingly. *Thank god my father went into business, not poetry. He's far too much of a romantic.* I laughed, incredulous at this portrait of my stiff employer, and Aida reddened. *It* is *romantic, if you think about it. He planted the grass for my mother. She's one of those Catholic Koreans, painfully devout. You know. The promised land, Canaan, found after forty years of wandering the desert. The land of milk and honey.*

She hurried ahead, calling to the dogs, who drummed her chest with oversized paws: still growing. Twenty and brilliant and motherless. *Down,* she told them. Sun slicked the horizon. Red fields, red fur, red cheeks; as they wrestled, one many-legged creature rose and fell through the reddish dust. I thought of Mars: the planet, the angry young god. *My heart,* she said when they went slack, obeisant. *My love, my darlings.* She looked up. The horizon threw out its final light show. Tenderness remained in her voice as she said, *You're shivering.* She lifted her sweater. Drew my hands to her skin. Her body ran hot and steady as the dogs snuffled around, a protective ring of animal warmth.

———

Like the air of that mountain she retracted, cooled, hardened. It never failed to surprise me: how quick the shift, how abruptly the long, lazy day fell off the cliff of night. Her face was stern by the time we began training the dogs in earnest.

We anointed lures with smelly oils and threw them. When successful in retrieval the dogs got a nod, a curt, *Si*. But when they failed, when they punctured the fabric that she desired they hold with soft mouths, she struck them.

That's how you end up with a biter, or a runner, she said, scornful of conventional methods. *Or, worst of all, a dog that fails at its most fundamental task: protecting its owner. Sentimental nonsense. You have to physically dominate.* She wasn't cruel; she didn't strike to injure, or out of fury, but her object was greater than their affection. *They cry as calves do when weaned. I'd recognize the sound of true pain.*

The yelps, performative, faded. Slate, travertine, quartz, the terrain against which glaciers melted: they were learning she can't be moved.

The dogs had mastered stillness by the time Aida opened her canvas sack. A live lure burst forth, black and furious, and for a moment I saw my cat—but it was a bird that flew in one line, unerring, that cut across the pattern of field, horizon, dusk, the great unsentimental order that Aida saw. By that same logic, the dogs, bending to a purpose bred into them, swiftly brought down their prey. She whooped them on.

Down the mountain, an answering call came.

A red shape flickered at the horizon. Not a dog this time—flame. By the light of a distant fire it was just possible to make out a man, sprinting for the border. He yelled as he went.

Italia, I heard. I turned to Aida for explanation.

This was no training gambit, I realized as the seconds ticked on. Aida stood canted at a strange angle, as if wanting to move, as if unable.

This was fire and it consumed.

I acted with the certainty of a dream I'd dreamed every night since the letter from California. What burned in the dream some nights was an apartment with white walls, or taupe, or yellow, or walls papered with money, a lifetime's accumulated tinder gone up in smoke. In some iterations, what burned was a hospital bed, and in it my mother's face. But more and more often what burned in my dream was the restaurant, sending up a smell of scorched strawberries; what burned was the green grass, and all that lay beneath. On this night, I was awake. I ran toward the flames. The dogs came with me.

I never liked those dogs. I disliked their cool gray eyes, their thought-less sense of belonging that I couldn't hope to emulate. I disliked how she bent toward them. Yet I was grateful for their closeness as I beat the flames with my coat. I felt no pain. Only the blazing, obliterating privilege of defending a place I had begun to dream of as mine.

By the time security arrived, swarming down from towers and up from hidden hatches, the fire was out. The grass had been too damp for real danger. I felt sheepish about my hue and cry, which seemed excessive, as did the force with which guards tackled the arsonist.

The strange man stood silent in the face of questioning. He was smaller than he'd looked from a distance, stoop-shouldered. With each passing moment he shrank into himself, one sleeve held over the swol-len mess of his lip. The gesture read as oddly demure. He seemed to bear no relation to the screaming figure who'd set the grass ablaze until Aida pushed forward.

That bloodied mouth released, at the sight of her, invective as explosive as a hand grenade. Aida jerked back from the vapor of his blast. I recognized the source of the arsonist's heat, if not his words. That same hate, mixed with envy, had fueled the Italian immigration officer who let me through to the mountain.

This man, when finished, did not stamp a passport. He spat.

Aida examined the bloody glob with dispassionate intensity, as if a specimen set beneath her microscope. She was still staring as guards dragged the arsonist off. Gently, I shook her shoulder.

You drive, she said.

She didn't wait for my response. She slid into the passenger's seat and shut her eyes to me. I had to lift her arm to take the keys from her pocket, a curious sensation, like touching a substance not quite solid, as boneless as a jellyfish's limb. Only her hands moved in the dogs' fur, and her eyelids. They twitched, as if watching something not visible in our drive through the darker, more quiet night.

But I saw.

I watched hundreds of fires this year, I said into the stillness. *It became an obsession after my apartment burned down. I'd get home, fill the tub, and just sit there, scrolling, until the water went cold. Name any structure and someone's filmed it, or rendered it burning. Technology, am I right?* She said nothing. She didn't have to. Her face without its sharp black eyes was naked as milk upon which every tremor shows. *What I mean to say is that watching helped. It's just as hard to miss disaster as it is to bear witness. If you don't see—you keep imagining.*

I had missed the burning, as I had missed the hospital's call. Two in the morning, end of my double shift at the restaurant in Paris, and I missed the call. The hospital didn't account for time zones, and didn't try again. My mother always said Los Angeles General was staffed by incompetents; I like to think that it gave her some comfort, in her last moments, to be proven right. Aida whimpered against the seat. The smell of smoke faded as I drove, adrenaline washing away to beach me on the shores of a feeling I'd brushed against the night we dozed to K-dramas in an empty restaurant. Private, somnolent. Peaceful. And like those fictive scenes playing back in a dark room, I knew for the first time that one day this tape, too, would cease to play its loop of my mother with her hands in the sink, my mother in a hospital bed, my mother dying alone without saying what I needed to hear. One day, I'd switch off the screen. Shut the door. A new me would walk from that room: I would live.

Aida opened her eyes.

Fuck. YOUUUUUU, she howled into the night, and I knew she'd be okay. *I won't repeat his nonsense,* she scoffed when I asked what the arsonist had said. *You heard him. He was loud enough to wake Belgium.*

I don't speak Italian. At all. There seemed no more space for shame between us. *Your father doesn't want me to learn. I guess he thinks it's a waste, given that he might not keep me on.*

He can have no more doubts after tonight. Do you know how much we would have lost if the fire reached the elevator shafts? If it got belowground, on that field— She wiped her eyes.

When I glanced back, the field at the base of the mountain looked as empty as ever. That night, I took for granted that the grass hid more labs.

Italy for Italians was how Aida translated the arsonist's message. She admitted that this wasn't the first such attack by nativists. Food had been stolen and construction crews pelted with rocks. A few years earlier, a far-right group had painted their faces with the colors of the flag and chained themselves to boulders. Because they refused to budge, a kilometer of land was ceded back to Italy. Hence the perimeter fence and the guards. *We learned our lesson—contractual borders counted for horseshit once the media caught wind of the protests. Though the government took my father's bribe, the hypocrites.* I asked what the protesters wanted and she gave a toss of her head that wasn't quite convincing. *Oh, simple demands. Just the Tunisians gone, the Bangladeshis gone, the so-called gypsies gone, and definitely the Americans gone. They even want the French and Spanish gone—that's how you know it's gotten serious.* She batted her lashes. *Me gone, of course. My father gone because he's a traitor and no real Italian now that they're petitioning to define Italianness by how many generations back a family goes—they got that idea from America, thanks. They'd wet themselves with glee if they knew my mother left of her own volition. They want their mountain back, whatever that means. As if any of them could make use of it as we have. As if they ever set foot here before the smog.*

Maybe they're hungry, I ventured, thinking of the food I threw over the cliff. *If we shared—*

She looked at me as if I were an idiot. *You think we didn't try? The real question is, what* don't *they want? We donated money. They want more. We sent food. They complained that it wasn't enough, and that they wanted— no, deserved—semolina instead of winter wheat. We shared our preliminary findings on a cultivar of mung beans that grow in the dark, and next thing you know the Italian government's sending an armored truck to commandeer our data. Years of work, gone.*

The gray, gritty, life-saving flour. *That was your team?*

She waved it away. *We were one of a dozen labs working on the problem. We didn't get far. Our objective was to breed a cycle crop that could be alternated with rice and squash, so as not to deplete the soil. The point is, we gave what we had willingly, and where's the gratitude? They broke the terms of our agreement and didn't let us complete our research. They used our work to* make another monoculture, another genetically vulnerable, absolutely disgusting—

That aftertaste—

Like cardboard—

Soap—

You can't bake with it, not properly, and if you try to fry—

Oh, trust me, I've tried.

We cackled with the hysteria of escapees. She seized my hand. *So you get it. The same systems and rationales that led us to this point, that have reduced global biodiversity by ninety-six percent in the last century— we can't cave to shortsighted demands. That's why we hide most of our animals and crops belowground. We bribe the officials to stay away, and we lie. They'd destroy our work if they found it. Give this land over to humans and it would be gutted, stripped, in a week.* She called forth a vision of heirloom beans thrown out or reduced to watery shadows of themselves, of Bresses slaughtered in favor of sickly industrial hens, of soil so depleted by mung bean monoculture that it blew away in clouds even thicker than smog. She stroked the dogs as she spoke, she slapped her thigh for emphasis, and though she grew hyperbolic, though at some point she mixed up the nativists and the government and all the people of Italy and I could not tell which she hated more, the simmer of her rage was intoxicating, heady, the surface of a broth about to boil and release its pungent scent.

Don't ask me to explain their twisted motives, she concluded. *I have better things to do. Why are you so interested in what they want, anyways?* I felt the weight of her gaze. *Aren't you sick of that?*

Of what?

Empathizing with shitheads who'll never see you as one of them. The words were harsh. The kindness with which she spoke them was like the sun as it blurred the horizon of the country each morning, a daz-zling eradication of what had come before. *So what if you can't get back in? America's doomed. Leave them to it. I'm building a better world for us, one that you saved tonight. I'll speak to my father about you.* She held my gaze with an intensity I didn't know I deserved, so that I had to look away. *I promise.*

How can I describe my life in the years leading up to this moment except in shades of gray? All the scrape and grind of it, all the empty shelves and lost ambition, all the soot grown hard on windows, season after season the only black harvest. The bad news, the debts, the visa applications, the flesh of your arm humping white between a nurse's fingers as she stuck you with a paltry twelve months' protection against whatever new strain of disease, as if bankruptcy or homelessness or a weariness at aping the motions of life weren't more likely to kill you first. My ducts were clearing in that country, my lungs pinkening, my kidneys detoxifying thanks to pure mountain water. There was kind-ness planted beneath Aida's scorn, soft loam under thorny cover of privilege. *It's not that easy to go home again,* she'd told me, and I'd taken it for pessimism. Petulance. Some things are easier to see in the dark.

Tell me more about the labs, I said. *There were two wings I couldn't translate.*

Her freckles, when she smiled, formed continents.

Charismatic megafauna was the term for elephants and golden chimps and their ilk, species prized by humans for symbolic or aesthetic quali-ties. Cuddly panda ambassadors had once prompted bamboo conserva-tion, and manatees had shaped legislation that slowed the destruction of Florida's Everglades. Nowadays, with extinctions a foregone conclu-sion and humanity focused on its own survival, charismatic megafauna were good only for impressing potential investors. Aida shook her head, bemused. *All those fuzzy species we keep around for reasons of ir-rational human sentiment.*

Like your dogs?

My dogs are functional, she said with cold fury. *A security asset. Let me drive.*

She took the road so fast that I couldn't form words for the wind in my face. We didn't speak again until she braked, hard, in front of the restaurant. Another fence post toppled.

I didn't mean it as an insult, I said, touching her arm. *It's obvious you love your dogs. Everyone is sentimental sometimes.*

The flesh of her arm was moon-bright on its dorsal side. It beat with a wild pulse. She was no longer angry. With great exhaustion, she said, *What is the function of love? I raised them and feed them. In turn, they protect me. Nothing more.* She said the strangest thing then, what rever-berates through the long hall of memory so that it is louder now than ever, a rhythm as much mine as my own heart's. *I'm not everyone. I can't afford the luxury of sentiment.*

It was only as I got out of the car that I remembered to ask about the final wing of the lab. Prelibatezze.

It means delicacies. She drove off.

The cat could smell the wider world on my skin. He perked, nosy crea-ture, into a semblance of his former self, nibbling at my shoes. Warily, remembering how he'd once happily barfed up yard trimmings, I of-fered a tuft of sedge. He accepted that. He accepted a bit of chicken. I left the door cracked to the wind. Both of our appetites were improved that night.

My employer called as I was eating. *Saved*, he said of the fire, and I demurred, thinking the two of them dramatic to the point of embarrassment, not yet aware of the extent of their desire for salvation, or of what lay concealed at the base of the mountain.

I require forewarning the next time you make such a visit, but I admit it is a good notion. You should see the seed labs next, I think. It's time you understood our greater purpose. He shifted the phone, and as the line crackled his voice went rough with static. It smoothed as he said, *I confess myself pleasantly surprised. It is rare that a candidate impresses my daughter. Your cooking has quite seduced her.*

Thanks, I said after a pause.

Your trial ends soon. Aida's promise moved through me like electricity. *I will address your role in due time. First, there is the matter of your health.*

I assured him that the burns on my hand would be fine. I'd suffered worse in kitchens. But he was referring to the doctor's assessment.

Take better care of your body, my employer warned. *This is a command, not a request. It is my desire that you live a good, long life, longer than you yourself might imagine. I can imagine it. I can assure it.*

I can still feel the curve of the phone in my hand, its weight. The cat could not nudge it from my grip. Aida had been right. It was the most romantic thing I'd ever heard.

Five

✼

I turned thirty. Having dreaded birthdays all my life, I discovered
the texture of my own contentment. Isolation ceased to unnerve
me that May. I settled into a lull of sky and sun, of existence almost without language, without the attendant agony of thought. No
alerts, no news, no front-page eulogies to hummingbirds or swifts, no
extinctions of nothing and no one I cared for. Pollen lay thick. In hidden fields, grains raised their heavy heads. Menus swelled even as the
stores of dried and frozen goods sourced off-mountain diminished; in
their place came deliveries bloodier, fresher, sixty then sixty-three then
seventy percent of meals sourced from the country's own herds and
fields. The bubble of privilege I'd scorned no longer seemed so bad if
within it were such spring eels, such endives, such reliable visions as
Aida's. I binged the third season of an insipid K-drama whose plot I
could, and did, predict aloud as I brushed the cat's increasingly matted
fur. He freed himself with a hiss, showing no interest in looking pre-
sentable. *Choose to be miserable, then*, I called after him. It would be ten
weeks on Sunday. For my birthday, I wished for permanence.

———

The menu that Sunday was a break from the usual rich fare, an ode to staple crops and fermentation. Amaranth tumbled, fat, in hay-sweet troughs. Olives lay curing against crags of deep-veined cheese. I was elbow-deep in garum when I heard the door open.

Taste the preserved lemons, I said without turning. *Tell me if they need salt.*

No, said a strange voice.

One rough syllable. Male. Something off in that sound. The only certainty was its current of violence. I picked up a rolling pin and looked around.

My employer, in a pale gray suit.

His cold black eye was as it had appeared from afar, his broad shoulders, his height. Nothing else. The distant image of respectable, middle-aged wealth was made a lie by movement. As my employer circled the kitchen, his gestures revealed themselves as stilted, self-conscious, his back rigid in the hypercorrect manner of those who studied confidence late. He'd shaved his face as well as his knuckles, yet stubble poked through. Was that makeup at his bronzed temples? A spray-on tan? Most disquieting was his voice. The vowels came coarse and jarring, cadences lumpen, the effect like a bag of rocks dragged downstream as he said, *Perhaps Aida has informed you that I lack the ability to weigh in on matters of cuisine.* No, I might've said, or Yes, it was hard to focus. A surreal quality stole over the sunny afternoon, as if, over my neat domestic scene, someone had switched on a horror movie's soundtrack.

He must have used voice-changing software on our phone calls. No wonder he preferred written notes. Inexplicable, grotesque, but there it was.

This will be tonight's main course, my employer said as he set a package on the counter.

Out of damp paper slid a length of meat, night-dark and slimed with the telltale signs of fermentation. The stench grated against the tender flesh of my nose; it took all my professional training not to gag. The paper bore a smudge of Cyrillic lettering.

Whale? I asked. When my employer failed to respond, I promised to seek Aida's input.

My daughter will not dine with us tonight. My mind leapt to disaster, an invader in her car, blood on the road— *She is traveling.*

I'll set the table for nine, I said. *Who's serving tonight?*

You. Keep ten places. You will join us at the table. Dress appropriately.

What? I mean, in what? As if I'd stumbled onto the wrong stage, lights overbright, missing my cue. I'd heard his voice before. Couldn't place it.

The white dress.

Off, he said when I reemerged. Beneath his gaze I stripped off the long silk gloves I'd found in the dress's folds. My bandaged hand spoiled the effect, but my employer only said, *Do the burns still pain?*

A bit. A lot. *Is this seal?* I'd garnished the mystery meat with lingonberries and lemons. *Walrus? Selkie? Kraken?*

He ignored my jokes and escorted me into the dining room. My silk sighed against the weave of his pants, elegant, atonal, unsettling. *I want you to play a game*, he said, and I thought of the notes that had led me up the mountain, of the dress awaiting my arrival, of the duplicitous electronic voice on the phone. The game had begun long ago. I failed to grasp its rules. *Tonight, you will not speak.*

Um, I said.

Nor do you understand what is spoken, not even in English. Your job is to serve quietly. Pleasantly, he stressed. *When the time is right, you will lead us in saying grace.*

Without speaking.

Yes.

So I just—pretend to pray?

Is that so difficult?

Giving up smoking had been difficult, picking seeds from four pounds of chilies was difficult. I'd worked at restaurants where we constructed sixty-dollar entrees from rancid fish, where we ignored the alcohol businessmen purchased for their underage escorts, where we refired perfect steaks without complaint. Admitting that I had grown comfortable cooking for the wealthy, that I no longer knew a greater ambition—that was difficult, at times. This? This game was an easy trade for permanence. I made the universal sign for zipped lips. *And smile*, my employer said as he led me into the dining room. He steered the small of my back. We entered in false intimacy as the guests looked on in shock.

They seemed determined to affect casualness after that first moment. The mood in the dining room was odd, buffeted by emotions I couldn't decode. Air kisses, brief handshakes, no attempts to speak to me: the guests had clearly been warned about the rules of engagement. A few touched me so gingerly they seemed to doubt my solidity, as if I were projection or ghost. I was reminded of the worker who'd fled from me in the storeroom.

Only one guest made an attempt to approach me. In the privacy of the women's bathroom, an English sheep heiress said, into my ear, *An-yeongseyo*. I recognized the Korean greeting from my dramas. I refrained from saying, *Wrong Asian*. Pleasantly, I nodded. She gripped my bare shoulder. Pleasantly, I did not shove her away. *I wanted to check on you, my dear. Are you well? We heard, that is, we believed that—*

Hush, said her half sister, peering around as if my employer might be crouched behind a fern. *You know she can't understand you.*

This, then, was the test of the other abilities my employer had alluded to, the night I proved my value outside the kitchen.

For the first time, I bore witness to the success of my meals. The cheeses I'd laid out oozed invitation. As planned, the tang of my accompanying giardiniera nudged guests toward the tannic relief of drink. I'd left wedges whole so that diners bumped shoulders as they peeled and sliced, offering tidbits to their neighbors. Discomfort slid into easy camaraderie as I stood aside, smiling. Triumph was headier than the liquor from which I abstained. I had steered the powerful by their tongues.

I ignored the voice that asked, hadn't I meant to feed anyone else?

The spell of food failed only on my employer. He sat with undrunk drink in hand, taking pleasure in nothing—not the sturgeon, not the Sancerre so crisp it curled the toes, and certainly not the company. Every so often a guest would turn, with an air of charity, to offer a joke or question to which my employer gave his curt response. Relief was palpable once this necessary evil had been done. Oh, he was an impeccable host on paper, pouring wine and complimenting sartorial choices—but he was stiff. False. Those unblinking eyes. Something lay behind them, something we were reluctant to uncover.

They didn't like him, or he them. His authority was built on fear. It occurred to me, much later, to wonder if he feared them, too.

Because powerful as my employer was, his behavior betrayed a note of almost childish hesitancy. He spoke a half-beat too slow or too fast, tripping on the heels of others' sentences. Or he'd thunder into a murmured discourse, causing guests to wince. Over the measured voices of that well-bred crowd, my employer's accent hung like an odor never quite dispersed, no matter if he spoke English or Spanish or French. Even Italian failed to sound like his native tongue. And so he said hardly a word until the appetizer.

I was spooning out the beans, cool in their bath of brodo, when my employer stood at his seat. He waited for cutlery to clink to a stop. Into that artificial stillness, he said,

——————— —————— *Saavedra.*

There was a beat of—nothing.

Polite interest, at best. Increasing bemusement as my employer repeated himself. Finally, the petite wife of a Swiss technologist spoke up. She'd drunk more and eaten less than the others, and her rudeness required no translation.

Redness tinted my employer's mask. Unblinking, unsmiling, he raised his voice to say more, at length, unconvincingly. The two English sisters traded looks. An Italian steel magnate fiddled with his spoon. Faster and louder my employer spoke, and I would not have guessed that his diners shared a common language. At last he turned to the sole American guest, fooled, perhaps, by the smiles the man kept flashing in a bid to ward off awkwardness.

Your industry is another that relies on scientific innovation, my employer said, switching to English. *Surely you understand the value of Saavedra's seed bank.*

Weee-ell, said the American pharmaceutical president. *I'd say Saavedra's greatest value is his friendship with Kandinsky.*

The room contracted. Even the rude Swiss woman leaned in. My employer smoothed his hair, revealing a suit gone damp beneath the arms. *Kandinsky has expressed interest. Nothing more is confirmed as yet. I do not trade in speculation, as all of you should know from the manner in which I conduct my business. Have I not proven that?* The question came out petulant, aggrieved. *Kandinsky is not the reason we gather tonight. What you eat at this table owes a debt to Saavedra and his seed bank.*

In the silence, a French media mogul picked up his spoon and let a single beige crescent fall. *Haricots pour bétail*, he said with disdain. I understood the word for beans right away; it took a second for my rusty kitchen French to decipher the rest. *Beans for cows.*

Fury emanated from my employer. He turned it on me. I, in turn, studied my maligned beans to the sound of the Frenchman complaining, now, about price. The beans weren't the most visually enticing of the courses, but they were appetizers for godsakes. Meant to whet. How could I have known that they would sharpen an appetite for my employer's humiliation, a hunger for—as I gathered from other diners who chimed in—recompense? The table was one moment from asking that their meals be comped when my employer gripped my gauze-wrapped hand. I flinched. *Serve the main course. Now.*

The dark meat had changed while it sat out. Edges deliquesced, skating the queasy edge between liquid and solid. The kitchen smelled like the inside of a carcass. The meat looked unsafe, and I still didn't know what it was, or how it might turn the mood in the dining room, unless my employer meant to end the painful farce once and for all by poisoning his guests. I pictured little seeping beads of botulism. But between food poisoning and my employer's anger, the decision was easy. I heaved the platter up.

The dining room was so quiet upon my reentry that I thought my employer had admitted failure and sent his guests home. As it turned out, he'd traded conversation for lecture. He paced at the head of the table where, I don't know how, three easels had appeared. His pointer moved over pie charts and bar graphs and scatterplots and charts of arrows that ouroborosed into one another and charts that spread over three pages so that he flipped his boards, demonstrating growing blotches of sweat. The timing of the meal was thrown off; no food remained on the table. The mood had shifted from party to stale conference room, basement AA meeting, abstinence talk for sullen teens—valuable topics doomed to fail before bored and smirking audiences. The Swiss woman's head rested on the back of her chair; she snored lightly.

She rose, and not peacefully, as I passed behind her with the main course.

A wall of scent preceded me, rank and feral and as out of place as my employer himself. The meat was so dark it seemed to suck light from the room, oozing a mushroom density of decay, dank earth. What guests recoiled from, my employer embraced. He set his pointer aside as I staggered to a halt. He just about licked his lips.

Saavedra ——— ——— — — ———, my employer said, smiling.

The Swiss technologist was escorting his gagging wife to the door. The American finally lost his grin. *Is this a joke?* he said. *I'm an easygoing guy, and I came willing to hear you out on this project, but I can take my capital elsewhere.*

I promised that your investments would lead to miracles, my employer said. *Tonight, we dine on woolly mammoth.*

An incredulous silence swaddled the room.

I am no tyrant. My employer removed his sweaty jacket. *You are free to give up your portion of the Siberian mammoth our crews exhumed, by good fortune, as they were digging up Saavedra's seed bank.* He folded back his cuffs. *I see this discovery as a sign. A warning, if you will.* Setting his wedding band by his fork, he said, *Before you choose to leave, first consider how many are willing to eat from your abandoned plate.*

You think you can threaten us? The American stood. *I'll call your bluff, yeah. I don't think you have any other investors lined up.*

Not investors. I refer to scavengers that circle our country. We are under threat.

My employer lay his hand over mine, as if to comfort, and ripped off the gauze.

I cried out as my wound, half-healed, tore open. I jerked my hand to my chest. With absent-minded ease, my employer caught my wrist. Pinned it to the table. Gave his guests the raw pink exposure of me.

Over that strange tableau rolled my employer's voice of stone and shrapnel. He took the story of the attempted arson and shaped it, enlarged it. The single man became many, armed. The injured lip jumped from arsonist to guard. The fire grew to cast flickering shadow over the table, and I heard enough, before my employer switched to Italian, to know that no diner would dare leave the room, or the mountain, that night. Threat bound them to that soil as my employer's charms could not.

When my employer clasped his hands together, I knew it was time for me to pray.

I bent my head. Moved my lips. No sound. The effect was eerie, immediate. Guests lowered their heads, closed their eyes. I kept mine open to meet my distorted gaze in the window. On that night, I understood that my job was to disappear in full view.

My employer dispensed with knife and fork for the main course. His shaved fingers were long and brown and seemed possessed of extra joints as he plucked, almost delicately, at the mammoth. He sucked dark gobbets from his knuckles. He picked between his teeth. He was at ease for the first time, unmindful of posture; I saw Aida in the way he hunched over his plate. As he pointed to the door with a stained finger, laughing at guests' dismay, I saw where she'd learned mockery, too.

The younger sheep heiress was the first to dip her tongue to the meat like a small, neat cat. The Swiss couple used spoons. *Can a guy get a burger around here?* the American said to no response; in the end, he ate. I saw the moment the diners' revulsion changed as raw meat does upon hitting the pan, as raw fish did once adopted by the famous and wealthy and white; I carry with me this image of how disgust becomes desire.

I don't remember the taste of mammoth. That is beside the point. Can you imagine a swallow from the world's last cup of natural gas? Could you bottle and turn to tonic the thunder of passenger pigeon wings? Have you heard of Cleopatra, who dissolved the world's largest pearl in vinegar and drank that astringent juice? As I forced the mammoth down, I pictured myself devouring the night sky as it hung in thick chocolate patches above the mountain, smog-free and luscious, rarer than anything on earth. No elk by that point; no monkfish; no mammoth but for the portions served at the country's high table.

Anyone who has fed the rich knows that, past a certain price, it is not a matter of taste, nor hunger.

Apice, my employer said when the plates were clean.

Apice, said the guests.

They raised their glasses to me.

Blame the burn, blame the flushing of my ducts and the cleanliness of my living, blame the recollection of an old, sustaining dream. This was my debut as chef, and when my employer squeezed my hand, I hardly noticed the pain. I was already crying.

Toilet tanks ran all through that evening. The clenched gut, the deep scouring. Guests came back emptied, shaky, radiant. Converted.

Later: the vacant kitchen, the lingering odor of the night.

My employer set two glasses on the counter when I returned from the bathroom. The mammoth had come up like an oil slick, and the liquor fumes didn't help. I told him I didn't drink as a professional rule. *Neither do I*, he said, pouring for the both of us. *This is a rare cause for celebration. Do you know, they called you the best chef in the world.*

It was the mammoth.

A word of advice. Do not bring modesty to a business transaction. The truth is, a meal would not have had the same effect were I to serve it. But you, in white, wounded like our own Joan of Arc—your tears were a stroke of brilliance.

Over his shoulder I glimpsed my indistinct reflection. I was down to maybe ninety pounds. *I'm not Joan, am I?*

My employer did not say my name. I can't recall him ever saying it; not before this night, and certainly never after. He slid a new contract to the counter. *The permanent position expands your duties, with a commensurate increase in salary. You will supervise meals from upstairs. You will oversee kitchen staff. You will say grace every Sunday. And you will let them think of you as Eun-Young.*

Bile in my throat. *So it was never about my cooking.*

It is the title you wanted.

My employer looked on, perplexed, as I laughed.

He would have known the joke had he grown up through an American childhood during which colors were bright and music upbeat and the next act always scripted; had he come to a moment when props, curtain, stage itself went up in flame. So much of what my generation had been promised disintegrated at our touch. Consider the friend, a painter of seascapes, who dreamed of affording waterfront property. On the day the levees broke, the Gulf flooded her studio and painted her walls with costly oils. Consider the friend who worked for six years at a company he hated on the promise of a sabbatical, only to be let go. The friend who complained about family reunions and lost every relative over the age of fifty to a virus. The friend who saved up to invest in a fund and saw her money dissolve like sugar on the tongues of bankers who barely got a scolding from the SEC. The life we'd been promised was a scam, the world a scam, the whole goddamn play a scam and there seemed nothing to do but burn it down as rioters did in Paris, New York, Nairobi—and then creep back through the embers because what other choice did we have? What other planet? Of course I'd ended up in the middle of another scam.

Tell me, I wheezed, *how many women have you offered this job to?*

Only you.

Bullshit.

He tapped the contract. *My daughter may enjoy your crassness in private, but in section twelve you will see that your new duties include presenting an unimpeachable public image. Work on that.* He named two chefs he'd let go in the trial period. Their names sounded Korean and Japanese. *Neither was viable once Aida took a dislike to her.*

Can you blame her for not wanting a fake mother?

She does not yet know of this clause of your contract. He frowned. *Regardless, her personal feelings are inconsequential. Once I inform her, she will understand that this, too, is a part of our work.*

I don't get it, though. Why Eun-Young? Why can't I be—myself?

He picked up his glass, untouched throughout dinner. He drank like a man dying of thirst. He drank like a man crawling out of the desert of his life. He drank and said, *My daughter claims this vision for her own. She can be a child in that way. It was Eun-Young's idea from the outset, and began long before Aida's birth. My wife and I met in paradise, or rather a tropical island that billed itself as such. She was on a missionary expedition, I on my first vacation. I relinquished a small fortune for a cabana advertised as heaven on earth. But the water was polluted, and rather than marine life, the tide brought in trash. The local inhabitants were degraded, shrunken down through the generations into beggars and small-time thugs, a shadow of a shadow of their ancestors. Eun-Young and I always debated the rightness of bringing life into a world so debased. Others called us extremists. We simply intended to make a better place for our child.* Against the glass, all around us, sedges shifted and sighed, rose and flattened, under the hand of the wind. *When my wife left, I considered myself well rid of her religion. It had become its own pollutant, I believed. At my daughter's urging, I built this country of ours on a bedrock of scientific evidence. Rational thought.* He glanced almost fondly at his charts. *As time passes, I see that*

Eun-Young had the right of it. For all my daughter's brilliance, she refuses to acknowledge that the business of our endeavor—the politics of it—are more complex, more intricate, than what takes place in her lab. To be correct is insufficient. We must convince others to follow. We must win faith. I guessed at that capability in you.

But I'm not religious.

Aren't you? Explain to me, why do you continue to pay your mother's medical debt?

I don't see the connection. I kept my voice steady. *If you must know, I don't have a choice. They won't readmit citizens with outstanding debt. There's a point system that determines my place on the waitlist once the border reopens.* Debt-laden, famine-choked America had instated a law that held children responsible for deceased parents' debts. I was sure my employer had heard the details from his investigators, but he was waiting. I rattled the terms off by heart. One point for being under thirty. One point for having no preexisting medical conditions. Minus three points for being of an "overrepresented minority," meaning Asian or Middle Eastern or South American or African. Plus two points for each generation that American citizenship went back, meaning none for me, the child of an immigrant. One point for good credit, minus five points for my debt bracket, plus one to ten points for a commitment to invest ready cash in the economy in various amounts—

And you still believe they will let you in? My employer's smile was too wide.

Well, as long as I—

You believe in the assurances of a government that lies about its role in creating the smog. You were born in California, yes? Surely you've heard of the agricultural experiments out there.

There's a conspiracy theory for every—

So you see, you prove my point. My employer sat back. *You believe in a country that does not exist as you imagine it, in a code of morality as fanciful as any creation myth. What do you call that if not blind faith?*

As if Italy's any better, I said, forgetting myself. *They don't give a shit about this agreement of yours. They don't respect you.*

It isn't Italy I swear allegiance to.

Fuck you.

As I rose from my seat my employer applauded, putting together hands so large I couldn't help but flinch. Even standing, I failed to match his seated height. *Brava*, he said, and his admiration rang true. *However wrong your facts, your performance of faith contains a kind of—* this word again—*seduction. I am not capable of stirring such emotion. They dislike me. Nor do they like Aida, much as they admire her intellect. My daughter and I stand apart. We need a third they can trust, someone sympathetic and of a background they respect. As you point out. In this case, religion will do. We need an Eun-Young.*

That's idiotic. I'm supposed to, what, just keep pretending to pray?

Yes. My employer refilled his drink with a clank of glass on glass. I had reached the end of his good humor. His eyes were a continuation of the punched-out sky. *I am well aware that I waste time persuading fools when the numbers prove our efforts a necessity. The lot of you, squabbling and hoping and recycling and dithering and complaining about beans. Do you know what happened to the world's first seed bank? Of course not*, he said when I shook my head. *Because you are silly, and shortsighted, and individualistic.*

The first seed bank had been a project of Soviet scientists who, after the horrors of famine, vowed to collect every seed and grain on earth so as to safeguard future generations against disaster. So committed were these scientists that they gave their lives to protect the bank from

Nazi siege. *That was a miscalculation. Because they died, fools remained.* The government forgot the famine, the mission. The seeds rotted in storage during a power outage. All the genetic material was lost. *Individuals are selfish—but there is no point fighting human nature. And so this job offer comes with a signing bonus. Converted to American currency, it is seventy-eight thousand, three hundred and forty-five dollars, and ten cents.*

The syllables crashed against glass. My left ear rang. It was the entire sum of my debt.

When I could speak, I said I needed time to review the contract. I needed a clause that allowed me to leave restaurant grounds. My employer inclined his head. Those black, black eyes. *And*, I said, *I'd find the offer sweeter if you rounded up.*

This time he waited after lifting his glass. *Whiskey was Eun-Young's preferred beverage for celebration.*

The mechanisms of survival are pitiless. There are times to eat when you have no hunger and drink when you have no thirst. Life, as they say, must go on, and go on, and go on, even when you cannot see the sense in it. I drank. The zeroes hit cool and plush at the back of my throat. As my employer described the Japanese practice of hiring actors to replace missing loved ones, from which he'd drawn inspiration; as I gulped my second and third drinks; as alcohol spangled my vision into soft kaleidoscope, I wondered how my employer planned to replace me should I leave. I saw a line of women in white extending through the glass and down the mountain, sharing one name, serving dinner week after week.

He broke off suddenly. *What is that?*

I turned. No women. *The cat.*

What species?

Street cat, I said after a moment. *A rescue.*

My mistake. Certain mountain tribes eat Burmese cats in the deep months of winter. They are said to be something of a delicacy.

As the sun mashed yellow against the frame of another relentlessly beautiful day, I opened my smuggled Italian-English dictionary. *Apice*, meaning apex, as in apex predator, a creature at the very top of the food chain and thus never preyed upon. *Can you believe this shit?* I said to the cat, who recoiled from my boozy breath. I imagined Aida's expression should she hear the terminology coopted for mere marketing. I looked up how to say seventy thousand. I yelled, *Settantamila*. The acoustics of the storeroom were such that my voice rang back rougher, burred, and I remembered when I'd first heard my employer speak.

Many years earlier, a video had made the rounds after a freak blizzard hit Europe in June. A private utility company had exponentially raised heating costs during the disaster, and an old woman was brought on camera to confront the company's owner. She named the sum of the bill that had wiped out her savings. She wept. My employer gave no focus-grouped apology. He forgave no debt. One or the other would have protected him; a lie would have protected him. Supply and demand, he said, according to the subtitles. *Seventy thousand is the market rate to stay alive.*

He was reshared and memed and autotuned, castigated by activists and peers alike. An easy villain, unlikable, with a voice to suit the part. This must have been when he bought the mountain and began to withdraw from the public eye. His wasn't particularly remarkable among white-collar crimes; it was just that he'd said exactly what he thought.

I read over my new contract.

A younger self would not have cooked under a false name. Might not have climbed the mountain at all. That self had hired herself out wherever, jetted off whenever, so certain there would always be a route back. She'd slaved and sweated and kowtowed and overlooked and overworked and made it to Paris without pausing to do her math, assuming it would balance out one day, the years of sacrifice against the coming joys. I was no longer she. I had learned the rude calculus of loss.

On that night, I counted up my eleven years in the kitchen, my eighty-six euros in the bank, my twenty-two cuts burns and contusions. I counted two or four or four hundred instances of racism and sexual harassment, depending on your definition: a frank squeeze of the ass, or a word, one syllable, hissed beneath a steamer's scream? I counted the extra shifts, skipped meals, chicken bones cracked for stock, their jagged honeycomb. I counted all I had sacrificed, lost. One job vanished when I complained to management about the sous who mapped each woman in the kitchen to a corresponding cut of beef. Two thousand dollars to the travel fixer who promised a seat on the last flight out of Europe to Los Angeles. Eight thousand euros to a restaurant that owed me back wages I couldn't legally pursue, having been paid under the table. A hundred and three dead in the riot that burned down my mother's apartment. Ten billion tons of produce blighted in the fields, plus all the tons yet to rot. The decreasing likelihood that the smog would lift, the years adding up to the truth that you can't go home again, my debt growing as nothing green grew, sixty thousand dollars become sixty-five become seventy-two. My employer had once named seventy thousand as the price of life. Doing the math that night, I suspected that, adjusting for inflation, he'd set the number too low.

It was a good deal. I signed my self away. Lives had been lost for much less than seventy-eight thousand, three hundred and forty-five dollars, and ten goddamn cents.

Six

✣

All these years later and you will still find those who speak
with longing of the dinners served in those lengthening,
ripening days of summer. Those meals of yolk and sudden
juice, of larks' bones crunching in the molars like the detonation of a
small star, a black hole that swallows and makes irrelevant, infinitesi-
mal, what came before, and what came after. The tongue is not the
brain, that fizzing, keening, forever dissatisfied thing. The tongue
speaks the transporting language of pleasure. This is how it was, former diners still say with hunger clarifying their rheumy eyes: how the
lights came on through glass and beckoned up the slope; how the scents
unfurled like scarves, now pale and soft, now reddening, richening, the
brandy so aged you could chew it and the meat so lush it was lapped;
how along with centerpieces of feathered swan and milk-poached year-
ling there was Eun-Young in clean white silk. With her thin white
hands of an ascetic she served the braises and glacé fruits and the napkins on which to wipe soiled fingers clean; and most of all she served
the assurance that this mountain was neither vulgar nor sinful but holy,
a return at last to the original garden where life could be lived without
shame in the sun. Those dinners, they sigh, the residents who survived

and went on to chair Nobel committees or amass collections of fine art, who debate the libretto of *Carmen* as avidly as cooks debate the best way to reheat pizza. Great minds still for the dinners Eun-Young served. Their eyes in recounting go heavy as fruit when it begs to be plucked; their tongues press forward.

And then the mind catches up, they jerk. Hands tremble back to laps. It is late in the day, the light dim, and as their own deaths, escaped, push in from the shadows, the survivors remember what came next. No, they correct themselves with terror or slyness or guilt or sheer animal elation. It was not Eun-Young, it was a trick.

But who, in the end, duped whom?

My directives, such as they were, boiled down to a new wardrobe, some photos, and one brief, instructive talk in which my employer's hands flashed down at my face.

The clothes arrived laid flat in wide, coffin-like boxes. Nestled among Eun-Young's silks and cashmeres was an album that showed Eun-Young at the piano, Eun-Young with a toddler Aida, Eun-Young in that white silk dress. The last photo is the sole souvenir I retain of the country. In it a woman turns left, off-frame. One hand clenches fabric. The remnants of a party can be glimpsed behind her, along with the torso of a man whose arm and hand end on her shoulder.

She was always in white. Wore the flat, hunted look of a woman who disliked being photographed. *She considered it a vanity*, my employer said as I turned the album's pages. His mask was unreadable; he and she matched. I got no sense of Eun-Young from these photos. Her face a puddle of milk. A cloud.

We looked nothing alike, a detail my employer waved aside. No resident of the country had met Eun-Young. The popular rumor was that she, very devout, had spent her last few years in religious seclusion. Vow of silence. We would build upon rumor so that our Eun-Young, in addition to producing no sound, would comprehend no English, Italian, French, German, Spanish, an image reduced to Korean, to Korean-ness, womanness, foreignness, piousness, blankness—

But, I said.

You are practiced in lying about yourself. My employer clapped me on the shoulder, a coach at a minor-league game. *It is an advantage that they cannot tell you people apart.*

It has always been easy to disappear as an Asian woman. *You people.* The number of times I've been mistaken for Japanese or Korean or Lao women decades older or younger, several shades darker or lighter, for my own mother once I hit puberty. *You people*, said the eyes of the annoyed barista who pushed a coffee I hadn't ordered into my hand, insisting we'd just spoken, that I'd wanted double espresso, low-fat milk. *You people!* cried the teens at LAX who insisted on taking my photo, certain they'd snagged a K-pop star in disguise. My favorite dinner party anecdote for many years was the saga of the willowy Thai hostess hired in a restaurant in bumblefuck, California, after I'd worked the kitchen for three months. She was model-skinny, towered half a foot above me in heels, and beamed pure hate in my direction each time a server addressed her by my name. She actually shrieked the day the chef threw a dishtowel and ordered her back in the kitchen. She couldn't handle it, quit a week in. As for me, I was learning too much, it was my first job, it wasn't worth my anger. I decided to be flattered. She was beautiful.

Aida, on our first day, saying, *You are exactly to his taste.*

I'd noted—the way you note the temperature of a room, or reruns playing on mute in a bar, details so mundane they don't command attention—that there were no Asian residents apart from myself and Aida. One light-skinned Black couple from France fielded frequent compliments in the mode of *caffè* and *nocciola*, hazelnut. A few well-tanned Colombians and Argentinians stressed their colonizing Spanish heritage. My employer was one of the darkest, though his hue verged to artificial orange and he wore so much makeup it was hard to tell. An advantage, I told myself as I studied Eun-Young's image. Over and over I folded the photograph to hide, then reveal, her face.

The photo in my possession has been handled to the softness of tissue paper. There are places where the light shows through. At some point, it tore along the crease; in my photo, the woman is now headless.

As Eun-Young I saw into the economics of a country that ran on the price of pleasure. So many millions for a residence on that mountain, so many millions more for a spot on the sunnier side, and millions upon millions more for a seat at the Sunday table, where riches were laid like lardo on the tongue, melting to reveal, at the body's heat, the acorn then the oak then the thrush of forest floor then the resonance of life itself, expanding. Who would not crave more? Who would not invest, if asked at Eun-Young's table, in research that produced such pigs and oaks and worlds lifted to sun-flecked heights?

On my first Sunday as permanent employee, I did not dare ask.

When it came time to lead prayer, I froze, unable to see what the diners saw when they turned to me, unable to see how I could be worthy of upcoming requests for investments in solar panels, geneticists, political bribes. My employer led me to the door with the air of a solicitous husband, making excuses about my burn. His tone was gentle, his hand on my back pure iron.

He smashed his fists to either side of my face as the door, heavy walnut, slammed shut. One sound masked the other. I felt the air pass over my cheeks, felt the wall vibrate. I had the distinct impression that, had Eun-Young's face not been an asset more valuable than her jewelry, those hands would have landed elsewhere.

Tell me more about her, I begged. *I don't know how I should act. Who I'm supposed to be.*

That is irrelevant. He leaned in so that the diners in the next room would not hear. His words came through rigid lips, deceptively quiet, bringing to mind the wind that blew in the abyss, and the scream it gathered as it was forced through the narrows. He said, *Think of this as a seduction.*

My shawl was woolly with Eun-Young's perfume. My employer breathed deep, as if gathering the strength to breach my stupidity. The cross between my breasts swayed as he said, *Religion is a flimsy construction of rituals infused with arbitrary power. The gestures have always been empty; behind them stand hustlers no different from you. All that is required is a convincing performance. Do. You. Understand?*

He held me in place as I made to rise. He hooked a finger in my shawl. Pulled it lower. *Give them what they expect.*

His hand lingered. Reluctantly, he touched my breast. I waited. Felt nothing. We both breathed out when he withdrew, as close as we'd ever get to the synchronicity of sex. A suggestion of desire hung between us, but it was a stale, mothball stench. We fit as poorly as Eun-Young's ring on my finger.

Still, reentering the dining room, I felt a delayed charge. A flush on my neck. A dark house, generator running, arousal flickering on through the half-gloom of fear. Under a man's hands—crush of his body—exigent breath—I remembered how to perform. Yes when I meant no. Lust or satisfaction or pleasure. Gratitude, as required, knowing that, naked beneath a man's disappointment, there lay this possibility of violence, as pungent and close-fitting as skin. One pound of flesh, paid freely, was preferable to a bloodier extraction. My past roles of sex kitten and hard bitch, blushing penitent, coy exotic, tease: I'd learned, long before this day, that I could play anything to avoid the role of victim.

My employer nodded across the table when he saw that I grasped his meaning. The woman I was to become was not a whole person at all. She was a hollow, a receptacle, a mirror held at a flattering angle. We understood each other: he, too, was not quite whole.

His psychological acuity surprised me. My employer was attuned to patterns of human behavior in which he could not take part; because he failed to be swept up in their currents, he could, from his remove, map the tides. He was a man who studied pleasure, and that summer I came to understand the particular variety he served. It wasn't tuna ventresca that drew diners to this community over others, nor was it heritage beef. It was the final bottle of a 1985 Cannonau, salt-crusted from its time on the Sardinian coast. Each diner had barely a swallow. My employer bid us not swallow, not yet, but hold the wine at the back of the throat till it stung and warmed to the temperature of blood and spit, till we wrung from it the terroir of fields cracked by quake and shadowed by smog; only then, swallowing, choking, grateful, did we appreciate the fullness of its flavor. His face was ferocious and sublime in this moment, cracked open; I saw if briefly behind the mask. He was a man who knew the gradations of pleasure because he knew, like me, the calculus of its loss.

To me that wine was fig and plum; volcanic soil; wheat fields shading to salt stone; sun; leather, well-baked; and finally, most lingering, strawberry. Psychosomatic, I'm sure, but what flavor isn't? I raised my glass to the memory of my drunk in the British market. I imagined him sat across the table, calmed at last, sane among the sane. He would have tasted in that wine the starch of a laundered sheet, perhaps, or the clean smooth shot of his dignity. My employer decanted these deepest longings, mysterious to each diner until it flooded the palate: a lost child's yeasty scalp, the morning breath of a lover, huckleberries, onion soup, the spice of a redwood forest gone up in smoke. It is easy, all these years later, to dismiss that country's purpose as decadent, gluttonous. Selfish. It was those things. But it was, also, this connoisseurship of loss.

In pursuit of that sixth, evanescent flavor, I served songbirds. I served the blossoms of the night-blooming cereus that flowers for one hour every five years. I served, to a skeptical German financier, hunks of pig trotter, ungarnished and surly brown, just the way the grandmother who raised him had served it, according to photos procured by my employer's investigator. Long after I served the petits fours and pu-erh tea (digestion) and arrow frog poison (purging and cleansing), long after others had gone home, the financier sat holding my hand in his big red paw and speaking of his dead grandmother, and potatoes, and, though my German ran out there, likely her lessons of grit and perseverance and eating the peels that had led him to name his company after her. I understood that I raised her shade on the plate. I saw my employer appear at the door. Close it softly at the sight of us.

That was not the last diner to cry at my table. The confessions I came to hear amidst smeared napkins and bitten crusts were charged with a near-sexual intimacy, for all that I touched only shoulders and hands. At first I did not, quite, understand the draw of this postprandial ritual, and why it ended in the cutting of a check. *You allowed him to invest*, my employer said of the German financier, and I marked the odd choice of words. Not persuaded, not scammed: allowed.

I served leeks of the crisp, sandy variety grown in the childhood garden of a banker from Andalusia. I served oysters, small and sweet as hummingbird hearts, once native to the south of Italy and now exclusive to my employer's labs; in the dead of that night I heard an Italian manufacturer wail over shells with an infant's inconsolable force. My employer's investigators provided the tools, but it was my hand that pried from each diner's chest the particular soft, wet muscle of their greatest desire, their deepest regret. Eun-Young's value became clear to me the night I served haggis. It was the younger of the British sheep heiresses who came to lay her head in my lap beneath a table strewn with crumbs of oatmeal, cooked blood. The arrangement startled me; we were almost the same age. In English she described her lifelong schism with her half-sister's side of the family: the clandestine upbringing by an unwed mother; her hatred for a father who failed to acknowledge her; a drab, anxious childhood of charity shops and free lunches, resentment sharpening her into an arrow aimed toward a UN career in poverty reduction; and the day her father died and bequeathed to her half a fortune accrued through the blight and exploitation of what had once been sheep country. She stepped for the first time onto her ancestral lands and saw hills scraped bare, the few remaining farmers mean, hunkered stones. She had intended to bring back the wildflowers and redistribute the wealth but learned, over years, how hard it was to divest from businesses that provided countless jobs in factories as distant as Turkey and Bangladesh; and how much proper reparations would cost for the exponentially expanded fourth and fifth generations of those original farmers; and how the descendants were so far removed from sheep and fields so as never to ask; and how little that cash, split among thousands, would mean, in any case, as the smog rolled in and dealt those hills their final death knell. *I'm not a bad person*, she sobbed. *There was no other way. I'm not selfish.* Whatever she saw in my carefully blanked face made her rise, lighter, to kiss my cheek. She left me alone at the soiled table.

I understood her words. I recognized her guilt: that choke in the throat, that disturbance in the gut, that nausea that slept with you woke with you would not cease. It had been weeks since I pictured the world below, the one in which Eun-Young had no part, but on that night new visions of blighted fields mixed with old hauntings of smog and starved children, a noxious roil. I sat for hours at the table with its melting butter and congealed fat, facing a roast boar still thick with gobbets of meat. By the time dawn honeyed the windows with its expiating light, I had conceived of no scheme to smuggle the boar down the mountain, pay the officials, hide the trail, grease the palms, secure the vans, without risking the country's secrets—without the meat going rancid first. I rose in my white dress. I no longer cleared dishes, having staff who threw leftovers off the mountain in my stead; nor could I stomach a single bite.

I started drinking. What else to do with my pointless mouth. One night I had too much and stood too fast and the room went blurry, my vision crowded with dark blotches. Suddenly I saw, seated among my diners, the voids of all their missing grandmothers daughters nephews husbands miscarriages beloved dogs horses childhood dreams Sunday dinners chicken soups ancient meadows youthful principles moral codes, and when I put my hand out to steady myself the darkness was eating through my wrist, too.

A little too much fun, my employer said, and I saw, as you see a black hole by a lack in the sky, the wife around whose absence he and his daughter had warped. The guests swelled around me. Steadying me, offering chairs and salts, calling for doctors, water, ice. Touching me. Wanting my touch. Greedy in the simple way of children for the assurance of my living body. Food power sex they could buy, but there is a reason the priest who expiates sins is called a father. They sought from Eun-Young the primal love of the mother who holds her children close, who says by touch of palms skin breast that she forgives them their past and their future too, that no matter what they do she loves them, she loves them, she loves them.

So many millions and millions and millions for a spot in Eun-Young's lap, where the final course she served was absolution. Oh, I scoffed at those who cried over stocks lost and wrinkles gained and deliberate infidelities, but to satisfy a diner you must make their palate yours and I could not, quite, hate them all. However privileged, however gluttonous, they had chosen this community above others in New Zealand and Hawaii and Peru because, small or large, they believed they had lost—they had all lost. The air grew oppressive that summer with the near-extinct flavors of Burgundy and beef, with the weeping caramel scent of the cannelés we baked from the recipe of the convent that invented them in 1482, the nuns now dead or fled, the cloisters empty, no more cars stopping along the road in Bordeaux for the enticement of sugar and prayer, all those old stones cracked, those ovens gone cold.

Naturally, my employer identified the price a person might pay to never again suffer loss. Even as they ate their eighth or eleventh courses, diners were reminded to safeguard their next meal. Their next. My employer understood, instinctively, the art of pairing oppositional flavors.

Over dessert he served graphs of declines and extinctions. Over creamy cheeses he displayed the scabs of my burn; or, after I healed, footage of skies curdled over with smog. Each week he poured out, with the Sauternes, an analysis of the souring political climate.

Rumors had spread along with the smog. Resentment of the mountain grew so great in even neighboring France and Switzerland that the Italian government had been pressured into scheduling an emergency referendum. At summer's end, the populace would weigh in on the government's response to the food crisis, including its support of the research community on the mountain. Whether the mountain should be permitted to exist, with how much independence and by paying what taxes, was a topic of speeches among the vying political parties. Luckily, certain politicians could be bribed to speak to constituents in our favor. Voting blocs in key regions could be swayed by well-timed gifts of food.

Investments poured in from the residents.

My employer looked for other ways to sharpen diners' appetites. He implemented Monday fasts for those who came to Sunday feasts, citing hunter-gatherer cycles of survival. He introduced physical rituals at which lesser investors could win a seat at the table; games of endurance, and strength, and flexibility and strategy and teamwork played out on the restaurant lawn. *Optimal,* he said as he timed footraces and sent recipes out for nutrient analysis. He served our success alongside the world's decay, an intoxicating flavor sweet with fear and rotted by pride. *Apice*, he said when he revealed that the average resting heart rate of residents was in the top two percent. *Apice*.

We are strong, he slurred in privacy as he indulged in the rare luxury of drink. *See how we make the blood of our covenant thicker than the water of the womb*. He burst into a fever of language that was not fully Italian. *La famiglia prima e ultima*, he repeated, eyes closed. I have not forgotten that phrase, nor the swooping drop I felt when I looked it up: the first and last family.

And so I ask who was scammed, and who the scammer. My employer's endless presentations, or those who clapped, then mocked him in private? My employer who called them family, or those who, in joining the country, abandoned their own? When I served bluefin at midsummer, every diner knew the dangers of mercury in apex fish. Yet they ate it, with shaved white truffle. Too much time has passed to say with certainty which of my employer's prophecies were exaggeration, which lies or heartfelt fears, what percentage malicious versus hopeful; and whether he knew, and when, that he was charting a course for disaster. Perhaps the better question is whether he himself knew the difference. As I learned that summer, to convince others you must first convince yourself.

To convince the cat was another matter. He puffed into a hissing ball of static the first time I slipped into Eun-Young's clothes and strapped on her ever-so-oversized heels. Scrawny, weakened, given to passing days in a sleepy stupor, the cat suddenly resumed his old habit of escape. He yowled to be let out of rooms Eun-Young entered, he the sole inhabitant of that country who regarded me with neither desire nor approval. *I should let you go, you ingrate*, I said when I found him trying to slip through the front door. *See how you survive out there alone.* Yet I could never quite lift the latch. Dislike knit us in that period, yet it was a mutual feeling, turbulent and deep, and it carved through the years as no other relationship did.

For the first time, I admitted that I needed him. Needed him despite, and because of, the sticky gaze of disapproval he'd inherited from his owner. *Who are you?* my mother had asked when she turned her back; I'd had an answer when I left California. Now I wore my hair impractically loose, as Eun-Young had, and coming down the hall at dusk my own reflection unnerved me from afar. It unnerved me up close, too. Who was the woman in the glass? Easier to answer as Eun-Young, she whose goals were her husband's goals, she who began and ended in a frame. Easier to slip on her silks than the tatters of my former life.

I'd hoped to find a sense of purpose with the kitchen staff. In front of them, I thought, I might grow into something neither the diners nor my employer saw. I'd worked under enough bad chefs to know that a good one concerned herself with more than food. I thought I might become instructor, leader, confidante.

I never had the chance. Oh, my staff gathered to watch my demonstrations of tying roulades or tweezing a garnish just so; but they studied only my hands, as dispassionately as they might a video. They took instruction but never asked why I sauced this way, the purpose of an overnight soak, my philosophies and job history, my hopes and dreams. If ever I deviated from the menu printed on my employer's scented stationery, I knew they'd direct questions to him. Language, which I'd overcome in other kitchens, was not the obstacle. My staff saw me as Eun-Young: an extension of the man who kept them in his employ.

And so I stood outside their jokes and intimate curses, though oddly, they adopted the cat. They fed him and teased his disdainful ways. He permitted such interactions so long as he was allowed to lick the nicotine stains from their fingers.

The staff smoked. It became a guilty habit of mine to watch them at their guilty habit; the spot they believed secret was just visible from the glass eye. Watching an ember move from hand to lip to hand, I felt a longing so acute it seemed it should cleave through the glass, releasing me, in a shatter, to reach for the cigarette. It occurred to me to wonder whether Eun-Young had felt what I did; whether she herself had fled to escape this version of Eun-Young.

I had the job I'd once wanted, but she who stalked the halls had no taste for such ambitions. I was another ghost evoked through fragrance and steam, but more than family country lands home lovers career I mourned the loss of myself: me.

My employer was monitoring a different sort of loss. One day he presented me with a new chart. On one axis: height. On the other: weight. He tapped a tiny area labeled *Eun-Young*, between a body mass index of eighteen and nineteen.

I warned you to mind your health.

At my height, the acceptable weight fell in a range of about two kilos.

I assured him I was doing great! The night before, a British car manufacturer had examined my face with disturbing skepticism, only to declare my nose job exquisite. Koreans had the best plastic surgeons, she said.

It's a joke, I explained when he failed to smile.

Eun-Young did not display so alarming a sense of humor.

In order to prioritize my conversion into a more ideal Eun-Young, my employer called my kitchen duties to a halt. *Temporarily*, he said. That word reignited the old fear.

And so I sprinkled my food with whey powder and swallowed capsules of fish oil. Without kitchen duties to distract, the images came more insistent than ever. My throat clogged with visions of grim restaurants, food deserts, Sunday smog reports, border patrols, a farmer's dead sheep, my mother picking clean the carcass of a Thanksgiving turkey. Her expression over the bird she'd roasted with neither brine nor rub was severe: no joy, no anticipation of delight, only work. Work. It was that expression I saw in my reflection when I emptied myself of Eun-Young: my mother who broke her fast on stale cereal and the non-moldy bits of moldy fruit, my mother who refused to eat my cooking, my mother who mocked my profession, my mother I mocked back for her dourness and narrow life of toil that I vowed to escape, my mother for whom food was sustenance and never joy: my mother who never knew pleasure. It was she I feared emerging from the glass as I found it harder and harder to eat.

I can see now that I was hungry for love that summer. For something to love: a bite, a dream, a person, a meal, a field, a piece of a world worth believing in. Not for me the solace of boeuf bourguignon; not for me red wine and browned butter, that unctuousness proximate to rot or burning that stickied a diner's tongue. I had lived too long in the low country. I had tasted bitter gray. Only ashes and lost empires in the crust of a kouign amann that would never shatter the same way again.

The cat sniffed. He, too, refused my plate. As he stalked away I was reminded of the lion in the lab, and the tawny rise and fall of its flank. That lion had been extinct for two years in Africa. This country had brought it back. Surely that creature was correct. Surely its continued existence was the crucible in which I might gather the remnants of my faith like broken glass, until I had enough to smelt anew, to forge something small but smooth. I pictured the passion on Aida's face as she spoke of gene editing and de-extinction, so unlike the echoes I chased in timeworn stews—her methods that were not recall, but renewal. The gleam of the lion's hide was that of the fine fur on Aida's forearms as she steered the car through the light in the hour just before sunset. I thought of her hunched over the plate, more fluent in her pleasure than her father for all his rhetoric, data, charts. Eun-Young was not flesh; she did not eat. But Aida did. I thought of her as I swallowed, chewed.

She came home on the summer solstice, the night of Eun-Young's supposed forty-second birthday. Paper lanterns dotted the lawn, waiting to be hung with charms and released, flaming, into the sky. Guests would be instructed to scribble down their deepest wishes. Later, unbeknownst to them, drones would collect the messages before they burned. Eun-Young's own stated wish was further fruitfulness, further goodness—in other words, further investments.

I stepped, staticky with dread, into my own party. Not a single guest noticed. They were looking at Aida.

She'd come armored as if for war. The shoulders of her jumpsuit: pointed. Her heels: spiked. Her hair was slicked into a helmet, black this time, no dye. It was my first sight of her among the residents and I was struck by the sheer performance of it, how unlike the person in her lab or my kitchen. The creature at the party was pure fabrication. It brushed its hair back with studied sleekness; it nibbled daintily at hors d'oeuvres; it emitted no whiff of dogs and dirt; it was cool, and knowing, and its top lip remained buttoned to its bottom.

She outshone me. She ignored me. I thought again of the Thai hostess I'd welcomed as an ally. Instead, close quarters had rubbed us into competition. To guests it must have seemed the oldest story: rebellious youth, a mother-daughter rivalry. But it scared me that I did not know the object orbiting the lawn with her father's eyes and his duplicity, distant as a comet, and as cold. I wanted to send her into free fall.

You're just like your father after all, I said when she deigned to greet me. My lips to her ear, so that guests did not see: the heat of my disappointment, my spurned and spitting need.

Pot, kettle, she said. *Fuck you.*

Neither was her reunion with her father sweet. I saw her shake her head at his questions until he broke away without an embrace, even one as fraught as mine had been. Aida stood alone, perfectly erect, until a guest called her attention. The lawn rang with her polite, fake laugh.

Residents looked to father and daughter for an announcement that did not come. Despite the veal braised in honey and leeks, despite the pâté en croûte cut tableside so that two hundred blackbirds inside began to sing, the air was redolent of disappointment.

I knew I'd hear about it. Inevitably, all woes came pouring into Eun-Young's ear. Once the buffet was served, I fled to the staff smoking spot behind the restaurant. I was chewing sedge, dreaming of a filter between my teeth, when the Iranian meteorologist stumbled into view.

Lucky me, he said with drunken satisfaction.

It was the first time we'd met in the flesh. Sunday dinners were for top investors actively courted by my employer; residents like the meteorologist didn't usually enjoy Eun-Young privileges. The meteorologist sat, intending to exploit his opportunity. *Cheers*, he said, and drew out a pack of cigarettes.

I hear you're the only person who won't rat on me, he said as I stared. *Your husband's rules about no smoking, no drugs, no fun, they aren't my definition of a charmed life. What's the harm of one cigarette compared to, say, predatory lending and embezzlement? I guess you people intend to keep your bodies as temples. Me, it's a little late. Sure you don't want a drag?*

I wanted the whole damn cigarette, wanted to rip the pack from his hands and run barefoot down the mountain poisoning my lungs at my own goddamn discretion. What I did was smile. Not quite pleasantly.

It must have shown. *Even our resident saint's got secrets, huh.* He dropped his face to mine. *I'd pay good money to hear a few. For example, where your daughter's been. People were beginning to speculate, the way they did when you went missing. Whether Aida was sick, exiled. Dead. Me, if I had money, I'd put it all on Kandinsky.* His voice sharpened, and I longed for the clarity of nicotine. *She must have gone to get Kandinsky on board. He considers himself an amateur scientist, so hers might be the shtick that wins him over. Looks like she failed, though. I can read the prevailing winds. It's part of my trade.*

I tried not to let my interest show. Very few residents—among them the meteorologist, the chief zoologist, the brilliant engineer responsible for the power grid—had not bought their way in. I felt kinship with anyone who'd won their spot by demonstrating a skill deemed useful; and whose presence was, therefore, contingent.

Kandinsky represents a stroke of either supreme confidence or desperation. They're all fixated on influencing this vote, but it doesn't count for much in the long run. Politics? He waved his cigarette dismissively. *Regardless of who owns the rights to it, this mountain has five, maybe ten more years before the microclimate shifts again. High-elevation steppes have gotten a pass so far. But look at Austria, look at the lower Kathmandu. The smog will spread. The sun will disappear. The grass will wither.*

Below us lay the spectacle of the night's Olympic-style games. Oiled torsos shone as men shimmied up poles, and women in brief tunics raced after a variety of golden, summer-ripened apple. It was a ferocious picture of health. For the first time I noted how young the residents skewed. The men were in their thirties and forties, with a decent minority, like my employer, in their fifties; their female companions, of course, ranged younger. Softly, ruminatively, the meteorologist said, *We're all dead in twenty years.*

One of the rare elderly residents walked to the cliff. She was the mother of the Italian actress, herself an actress in her day, and her profile was striking as she tipped her head to the sky. I didn't see her beauty then. I saw her varicose veins and fragile bones, her terrible aloneness against a night that shrank her down to a last of her kind. I understood what drew me to the meteorologist. Though shaven and respectable, he shared a streak of pessimism with my old friend, that supermarket drunk.

I suppose the meteorologist's prophecy should have terrified me. I felt only dull weariness. That gray. There I was with all I'd once wanted literally at my feet, the restaurant a platter from which I could pluck choice tidbits, the crowd ready to sing my praises—but what did it matter when I couldn't enjoy it for myself? When I didn't know what I enjoyed, or who I was? On that night, confused as to where I ended and Eun-Young began, aching from my dismissal by the one person I'd counted on to tell us apart, I saw us on the mountain as dinosaurs: slow dumb golf-ball-brained hunks of meat chomping placidly through our meals as if doom were not already set on its collision course, as if we would not soon cease to exist except as lumps of carbon.

Unless we move again, the meteorologist said, stretching. *We can keep creeping toward the poles so long as some government is bribable. Up and up. Some of us, anyways. Hey. If I say pretty please, if I write another report on my contributions, if I get on my fucking knees, will your husband take me with him when he goes?*

The meteorologist's smile grew desperate, sly. *Or is it you I should convince?* He touched my waist as men had done all night, that unthinking, casually appropriative greeting dispensed as freely as wine. *You can't possibly see anything in your joke of a husband. How about—*

Aida appeared like a miracle. Fresh white tunic, flushed cheeks. *Can I borrow my mother? It's time to cut her cake.*

The cake was not the one I'd baked as an afterthought. This was a foot high, silky yellow, sighing under the knife. Like nothing I'd tasted before. Part air, part kiss of milk and honey.

It's a soufflé cheesecake, Aida told a guest. *Very popular in Asia. I'll let my dear mother tell you its name. Korean is so stunning.* She turned to me and said something in that language, her face a beautiful trap.

I wrote on a napkin, spelling the words phonetically.

Kkeojyeo anyeongseo, Aida read aloud. Her lips parted. She excused herself.

A few minutes later, baying came from the restaurant, ragged and wild and unmistakable for laughter, if you knew. ———? a guest asked uneasily. —————— *perras* ————, my employer said. I recognized the Spanish word for female dogs.

I found her asleep in my bathtub, bare feet on the rim, tunic showing a wedge of freckled chest. The dogs stood guard while the cat spat furiously from above.

Manners, I warned him.

What a hypocrite your owner is, Aida said, opening her eyes. *Look what she brought us—what did you call it out there, Korean fuck you and hello cake?*

It looked very much as if the cat were smirking.

Aida chewed open-mouthed as she brushed off my attempt at gratitude. *I didn't rescue you. My god is that Iranian a pain in the ass, though. The engineers hate working with him.* She grinned, wolfish, through a mess of sugar. *If you tell my father about tonight, he might just throw that bastard off the mountain.*

Should I tell him?

She sighed. *No. The Iranian is essential to the plan.*

What does it matter. We're all going to die on this mountain soon enough.

Someone's been talking to you.

Is he right?

She slumped back against the tub, loosing the strain of her performance of a well-heeled young lady. *I won't let that happen. Have a little faith in me.* When I did not respond, she said, quietly, *Don't you start, too, not tonight. He told me I failed him. In front of everyone. All I need is more time.*

Because you have a grand plan that'll save us all.

Yes. She did not match my bitterness, my sarcasm. She looked at me straight on, a look terrifying in its directness, a look such as I had not experienced since donning Eun-Young's clothes. Gone, her cocky immaturity. She could summon an expression much older than her years, her gaze not flat like her father's but the black of metamorphic rock, a substance alchemized by pressure into something strong and obdurate that recalled the magma of its formation.

Are you telling me the truth? I asked.

Yes.

A touch: so fleeting I might have imagined it: her fingers on mine. She ran hot, as she had on the field. I did not want to die, it occurred to me as my blood pounded through my body. I did not want to go up in gray dust as the meteorologist predicted. I wanted to live. *I believe you.*

I can't tell you more than that, she warned. *Not until plans are set.*

I was sick to death of plans, plots, rituals, machinations, games. *I'm sorry,* I said. *That's what I should have started with tonight. I wish I could have told you about my contract in person. We decided this made sense. That is, your father and I—*

Aida stabbed at the cheesecake. *Don't. Just—don't. God, you sound like you're auditioning for the role of my actual mother.* Her fork ricocheted off the plate. Neither of us moved to grab it. *I see why my father wants you in this role. He's been hounding me to cozy up to investors, but you're much better at smiling along, shutting up, hiding what you think. My father believes you make us look normal, more like his bleaters. A sweet, pious little family. He wants so badly for them to love him. Do you?*

What?

Love him.

I hesitated.

With clinical precision she said, *Do you intend to breed with him?*

Jesus, Aida. No!

She resumed eating, with her fingers this time. I perched warily on the tub and snagged a bite. The cake was light, its flavor so evanescent that I took a second taste. My stomach stayed quiet. I dared a third bite, bigger. The cake was delicious.

It came out well, Aida said, pinkening. *Even though I shaved two minutes off the bake time. It's harder than I thought. Cooking, I mean. I missed eating your food. I missed—*

Terrines. Perfect roast chickens. Frisée aux lardons topped with the orange yolk of the country's eggs. As we spoke of Aida's experiments in gougères and amaretti, we slipped into the groove of who we'd been to one another, employee and employer's daughter, diner and chef, and it was a relief; I could not ask for more. Until she paused, midway through describing her failed experiments in sourdough, and said, *But you know what's more frustrating than natural fermentation? You.*

She shoved a finger into my chest. *Even now you're not saying why you took this contract, what you're thinking, what you're doing with my father. What the fuck. I come back and see you running around in my mother's clothes? You look stoned, or high. You've got this creepy, dead-eyed smile. My father says you won't eat. Do you have a disorder or what? Do we need to talk?*

How terrifying, how thrilling, to be seen. My skin crackled from the lightning strike of Aida's regard. I wanted to blush, cry, laugh, deny, admit, thank her, feed her, tell her everything and nothing, vomit into her lap my heart, which surely she could hear beating out of my chest. *Tell me,* I said. *Those people whose nerves were damaged by chemicals. In Baltimore, or Providence. Did they ever recover their sense of taste?*

What?

I've been missing you.

Her finger trembled. I hadn't seen snow in years, but I remembered it in the cream on her cheeks. That bright, pure ferocity. How it could blind you. But this was a land of extremes, a land you climbed to its peak and damn the cost. I wanted to live. Her face, a lifted plate. I bent to taste.

Seven

❦

June, July, were lost months. A breeze swept down over Europe, a polar vortex by way of the Arctic Circle that rendered mornings misty, diaphanous, the sky a soft veil behind which I split. There was Eun-Young in white, my employer's creation; and there, naked in Aida's arms, was a new self I met for the first time. There was the gray past and there was the present blooming blue out of those afternoons, those serpentine nights, the one long summer day that was Aida.

I'd starved so long I feared my own hunger for a wolf at the door. She let out the muscled animal of my tongue. Panting, teeth small nipped stars, she switched off the light. In the slippery dark of her I dissolved, no troubled body or changed face, only this fall through touch, through taste, through scent and breath and pulsing absolution of night, and: Yes to oysters swollen through butter. Yes to thighs cooled on glass, my hand a hot knife between. Yes to prosciutto, its salt slick; to avocados bursting, ripe. Our teeth clanged. I tasted blood and chocolate. Yes to the fatthicksweet of it, to cream, to froth that rises, to the crunched lace of the ear and the tender behind the knee, to that join at the legs where she softened, dimpled, begged me to bite. Three years, can you imagine, gray days and gray nights, no lovers no family no feasts no flights no fruit no meat and suddenly this largesse of freckles down her torso, this churning, spilling free.

I lost interest in food once before. Right after my mom died.

It's the half-light of early morning. Against a still-dark sky, this emergent landscape of her body. Lunar dunes, slick valleys, her throat a shifting topography as she asks, *Why.*

The ugly taste is on my tongue. Years of swallowing this. Years of gray. Denial and survival, survival and denial and suddenly I can choke it down no longer. I spit what's rotted.

I thought, what was the fucking point? I was supposed to prove her wrong. But the bitch never ate my food.

Her body moves away; I have lost it. In my mouth, the stale taste of lonely years. Then her face is swinging above, pale moon, and onto my stinging tongue comes her own, warm as grace. *Shhhh,* she says. In the close confusion of dark her words fill my mouth, yeasty, her voice pulsing in me like a secret my body has yielded on its own. *I'm going to tell you this just once.* Into my lips, my neck. Into the shivery space between my breasts she tells this story of the hunger strike she enacted the day her mother left, a child's belief in penance that ended when her father came in, crying. Into the basin of my stomach she names the wonders he gathered, fine shawls and rare perfumes, favorite books and cherished movies, a bowl of ripe persimmons. *And a camera to photograph me.* An image of Aida to be sent with other offerings. And her sudden realization that the woman who left was no god. Was unworthy of genuflection. *You don't need to prove yourself to anyone.* Into my thigh this ripe weight of her cheek. I close my eyes, taste juice. And then? I remember to ask. By then the sky is lightening, sun candescent at the hill of her shoulder. Dreamily she says, *We ate the persimmons. They were divine.*

That was the most she'd say of the woman who left her. A bowl of fruit, a father and daughter united in new appetite. After? I met she who leapt forth as if born like Athena from Zeus's head, full-grown and steely-eyed, the world her dominion. *Enough wallowing*, she said the next time I broached the topic. *Stay here.* Her fingers greedy as they guided mine to what was sweet. Her face, alive with her own pleasure. *Yes, here. Here.*

I had no kitchen duties in those months, and Aida no orders from a father gone silent since her ignominious return. When I asked, after a string of nights, about her going home, she shrugged. *A bed is a bed.* And then: *I prefer ours.*

We make our home the mountain.

In hidden orchards the stone fruit ripened so fast that what we didn't eat was given to the animals, and so like chimps like finches like gilas we glutted on plums so ripe they split if looked at, cherries and blackberries staining our sheets. We distilled summer meads heady with anise and yogurt, and watered fields with the barrels' dregs. To the tidal boom of an underground aquarium, I cut a sturgeon nose to slit and ransacked its body for that other fruit, pure caviar. I looked to Aida for the salt. Sweaty, unshowered, her pubis its own rough ocean. Saline, the meat of her as she bucked against my tongue, split open, gleaming.

My appetite returned with a vengeance. I craved the fresh. What was novel. *We aren't running out anytime soon*, Aida teased when I scraped the pan, licked the bowl, wanted to pluck from every bough in every orchard and run my tongue to the borders for every last drop of juice. The residents' meals came to evoke a sense of pity, a low-grade horror. Those ancient sauces, as suffocating and morbid as mausoleums. *Oink*, I whispered at Sunday's table, the only time my presence was still required. I disguised my laughter as the sobs of the devout.

My employer said nothing. He was occupied with the upcoming referendum vote. Talks with our allies proved so successful that my employer spoke of the possibility of parliament ceding another few acres to our country. Several Sundays saw tinted cars pulling up to the restaurant, disgorging politicians whose blindfolds were removed, with a flourish, at a table laden with just enough to entice. Their constituents, these politicians promised, were certain to vote our way. I paid little attention. As my employer had said, my job was to nourish Eun-Young's body: to eat.

This was the summer of my de-extinction, of life streaming back to its source. In the cool deep of the labs I witnessed the birth of the first Tasmanian tigers. There was an anomaly, a breech. A cry from the beast. *Mrs. Dalloway said she would buy the flowers herself,* said Aida, plunging hands into the birth canal. *You can't,* said the chief zoologist, a man forty years her senior. She was wet to the shoulders with blood and amniotic fluid but her face above remained composed, a face a sculptor might itch to immortalize. Medusa in her awful beauty, or Gaea, mother of Titans. Judith above the bloody head of Holofernes. The cub came free. Scientists swarmed with oxygen, monitors, tubes, but Aida put her mouth to the tiger's until it breathed: alive. Only then, stepping out so as not to disturb the animals, did Aida confront the man who'd ordered the cub be left for dead.

Life is not so profuse that we can afford to squander it out of fear or laziness, she said. *Which is it in your case?*

You risked the mother's life, the zoologist said. *You fail to understand the delicacy of these considerations.*

I understand that she was in pain. I understand that you are redundant.

Hubris, he breathed with the whole room listening. *You are as insane as they say. You may be clever, but you lack experience. These methods are reckless. They'll cost you in the end.*

She fired him. This, I thought, watching her face crumple red. Not the calm, not the constructed beauty. This was the face I would build a monument to.

Or this face, the day she brings me a pomegranate. She is clumsy. Shy. We've been reading old cookbooks, Greek and Roman, and food leads back to myth. I mentioned that pomegranates are my favorite fruit.

Binding me to the underworld? I rip the peel.

As if you'd want to leave.

I swallow not four seeds but every one she gave me. She gave me the secret of the pomegranates' prodigious growth. She gave me custard apples, loquats, damsons, songs of vine and hive and drives through sun-drenched afternoons when time hung suspended in amber. She gave me the sight of endangered starlings wheeling through a dome deep within the earth; I can still see their tessellations if I close my eyes. It took my going underground to see worlds greater than mountains than countries than nations I'd known, worlds insensate to borders and the small arithmetic of human life, worlds endless as sky and intimate as the musky den of returning home, that summer, to my own body.

With eyes adjusted to underground dark, I saw the possibilities that swim through grayness. I saw a more teeming and fruitful world I could love, that could love me. She gave me back my faith.

Persephone was no fool, I realized upon rereading the myth. Aida asleep beside me, her breath sour and sweet. Imagine Persephone for the first time in the absolute intoxication of dark, her senses stretching languid, the cave as moist as lover's breath. The feast, the chair, the plate, the fruit: red. Imagine a story whose moral is mute desire.

In the midst of that charmed summer, I was unsurprised to learn that the smog was shifting, too. Residents gossiped endlessly of how the polar vortex pushed patches of gray offshore, over ocean. My employer's ban on outside communications went forgotten as his power, derived from fear of shadow, weakened with anticipation of sun.

And so when he began to speak of the need to secure one or three or seven percent more votes to allow for a margin of error; when he described riots in southern Italy and the rise of a new ultraconservative party with a nativist bent; when he warned and lectured and foretold, residents raised sweet, glazed expressions. It was too hot for much beyond cocktails and finger food and talks of trips to Iceland, New Zealand, Argentina.

Suddenly we were all weather wonks. The Iranian meteorologist returned as the guest of honor one Sunday. Diners, rapt, followed his explanations of air currents and chemical reactions in sea foam. Only when the meteorologist warned of the smog's unpredictability did the conversation segue to iced drinks. My employer glowered; the meteorologist took more gelato and shrugged.

The day I heard news of sky glimpsed over the coast of Oregon, I excused myself to stick my hot face in the fridge. Scallops, leftover egg whites, vanilla, chicken stock, dulse and agar: I picked up a whisk.

Aida called them meringues later that night. Screwing up her mouth, she asked if I'd mixed up sugar and salt. I urged another bite. *What does it remind you of?*

Alarm, confusion, disgust flashed over her face. *Needs acid.* But she panted on hitting the white pepper, and I saw the kelp gelée slap her like an ocean wave, a briny awakening. *It's damp,* she said, straightening. *A bit spongy. Foamy. It reminds me of spit. Have you seen the bubbles that mollusks make when they breathe on the beach?*

I hugged her so hard the remaining bite was crushed between us. My explanation came garbled, but what were words compared to this transfer, tongue to tongue, of Pacific sea? She suggested citric acid and xanthan gum for my next batch, then left me to it. *At least you're doing something with the news. One freak reprieve has those fools ready to jump ship. False optimism is exactly what got humans into this mess.*

I was too giddy to point out that she was human, too.

Aida of many faces. I never tired of watching what broke, in private, through her softer loam. Her face blurred with lust, or distended around an entire duck neck. Her mouth wrinkling at the taste of sour, a flavor she disliked almost as much as bitterness. She championed, yet couldn't personally tolerate, escarole, kombucha, pure nibs of cacao. Her palate was at root a child's, craving the rich and the sweet. This embarrassed her. Was a failure of public image. Before residents she sipped peaty, eighteen-year Scotch; in the kitchen I kept a jug of sangria à la Aida, half juicy young red, half satsuma squeezings, with plenty of syrup and Calvados. I slipped sugar into her espressos while she held forth on fashion and genetic drift. Yet that wrinkle persisted.

It's the new inspectors, she admitted. To quiet grumbling from not just nativists but, more recently, the socialist left, the Italian government had begun sending surprise inspectors up the mountain. At each sighting of an official vehicle, shutters closed over the underground fields and labs, grass drawing smooth like a rug. Again and again a phytologist was trotted out to explain that the mountain's composition proved too thin and alkaline for quick results. Out came soil samples taken a hundred miles to the north. The lab's true progress stalled as these searches deprived hidden crops of light.

On orchard visits, Aida spent less time picking and more time speaking to researchers who drew her aside. It didn't surprise me when her father summoned her back to her work. What surprised me was my anger.

He's willing to talk to you when he needs you. I watched her dress in the predawn. *I thought you didn't have to prove yourself to anyone.*

I've nothing to prove. We trade resources, that's how the project runs. Give me a kiss. She yanked my chin back. *A real one. Like I'm going off to war.*

And so I sent her off with jars of terrine and crostini, with berries injected so as to pop on her palate like summer itself. I would render her messy, laughing, wiping juice from her chin. *Every artist must have a muse*, the pastry chef had said, but mine was not always around.

It was the cat who emerged into the kitchen near the end of the summer. Banished from the bed where Aida complained of non-hypoallergenic fur, he'd been banished, too, from my thoughts. The kitchen staff had taken on his care. After so long, I was shocked to see the new tentativeness to his gait. His fur was dusted white by the flour sacks on which he slept. He'd aged. *Poor bastard*, I said, and he lashed his tail, seeming to say there were better apologies.

I offered the newest batch of scallop-agar batter. To my surprise, he licked the spoon. I'd had Oregon in mind, but as the cat ate I recalled the beaches of Southern California. I knuckled down to his level. *Less salt, right? The water isn't as briny down south.*

And so it was the cat who bore witness to my experiments in those hours empty of menus, of diners and staff, of Aida. My scallops came out more saline as he watched, or frothier, or wet. Were they good? That's beside the point. Once, I heard a journalist say she did not know what she thought until she wrote it; I didn't know my own mind until I tasted. More than Italian than French than German that summer I learned a vocabulary of beaver fat and dulse, of dormice and powdered duck bone, of a tongue cupped to the tones of vanilla, acacia, green peppercorn. The cat yowled unless permitted to investigate each bowl. I'm not so crazy as to say I cooked for a cat—but in the wake of particularly disastrous failure, it was often his gaze, appraising, that spurred me back to the stove: the idea that I might, this time, finally stir his appetite.

He'd never been my pet, never a creature I chose for adoration or protection or succor. The murky waters of our past ran stranger and deeper. Yet he'd been there when I left California, and been there, and been there, constant witness with lamp-hard eyes. As the lit island of that kitchen floated through summer's indigo haze, as I cooked my way to understanding the person I was to become, he became, too: my kitchen companion. To this day I will turn at a certain shape of shadow, an inkling through a closing door, as if I might find him waiting just past the hallway's gloom. His previous owner had worked night shifts. Perhaps we were seeing one another's true natures, obscured all along.

Eight

❋

In August, when the heat reached its zenith, when what little wind that blew carried the overwhelming honey of sedge grass, when I served gazpacho after gazpacho and protesters broke into the Roman capitol to enjoy a little air-conditioning, the milk ran dry. My employer called past midnight to instruct that butter be taken off the menu. *Which menu?* I asked, yawning, and he said, *All. This Sunday will be the last.*

Aida explained with reluctance when I got back into bed. A lab tech had been granted authorization to visit family outside the country. Upon his return on a day of record heat, he neglected to trade his sandals for the lab's regulation boots and so tracked in dirt contaminated with a novel strain of foot and mouth disease. The tech had never entered the dairy himself, never seen the stately beasts in all their colors; his security clearance was so low he failed to understand the gravity of his actions. Questioned, he'd grown defensive, suggesting that it was the protocols that were flawed, not his own behavior. The entire herd would have to be slaughtered. There were frozen cow embryos, not all was lost—but no fresh milk for a year.

Why did you hide this from me? I said.

I was trying to protect you. You take things too hard. Yet it was Aida who struck her forehead with a closed fist. *It's my fault.* Thump. *I can't*—thump—*can't*—thump—*can't*—thump—*fail again.*

Any anger I felt at being kept in the dark evaporated. I held her wrists as she blamed her permissiveness, her neglect of the lab, her trust in fallible human staff. She delivered doom and gloom while I thought: What a relief to leave off cream in this heat. I asked about macadamia milk.

Macadamia milk, I repeated. *Years ago, I read about a spot in San Francisco that served it over charred root vegetables, in place of crème fraîche. Darling, don't you see this is an opportunity? Forget cows.* I kissed her palm. *Let's try it.*

Now?

The macadamias were buttery, fragrant, thumb-sized. I didn't quite nail the texture of the milk. My thoughts kept humming as Aida dragged me away. *Seaweed extract*, I murmured in bed as she, from her side, said, *I'll tell my father to end outside visits for the staff.*

She turned and slept, problem resolved. I lay awake thinking of the botanists who'd grown the macadamias, and the field hands who'd plucked the nuts. The workers who sang as they shook the pomegranates. A line cook who, in quiet moments, cradled the cat in his arms like the niece he rarely saw. The cat, prickly, permitted this. I was lucky to be in a different position from the rest of them.

It was the staff I thought of again when, days later, the results of the emergency referendum were announced. In a surprise upset, a grassroots organization of far-right nativists and far-left socialists had swept the vote. This party, so new it lacked a name or seats in government, was united under a common cause: the equal distribution of all Italian resources to Italians.

Yes, the voters said when asked whether the government should consider seizing private food stores above a certain size. No, they said when asked if the research community on the mountain should exist in its current form. An informal poll showed that nearly sixty percent would consider joining the new political party.

My employer rushed off-mountain to press his case with allies in parliament. He was not the only one. While he brought caviar and cash, the new party's leaders offered something more enticing still: survival. Already they spoke of sweeping next year's parliamentary elections, of voting out incumbents they branded traitors. Hypocrites.

And so there were rumors of legislation to seize land, or expel foreign aliens, or police borders more heavily. As we waited to see how popular opinion would translate into law, I wondered about my staff. As in every kitchen, they were darker than the diners they served. I had no idea of their visa status—or if, should they hold Italian passports, that fact would matter to the nativists. I lingered in the kitchen, wondering if my staff chattered less, seemed morose—but I couldn't ask and what was I supposed do? Pray? I left them to their work.

I don't know what I would have said, in any case. Sure, we might have shared disdain for nativists over a cigarette. But what would my staff have said about legislation proposed to increase taxes for the top two percent, to set up regional food distribution centers, to start a national seed bank by making it mandatory that all Italian growers surrender twenty percent of their viable crops? A year earlier, I would have voted yes, too. I did not know what I would say, who would speak out of my mouth.

———

On Sunday we slathered brioche with cultured butter, dolloped crème fraîche on daubes, and spooned a pudding of Aida's creation. The interior was so creamy it recalled the molten center of the earth. If the land of milk and honey produced no further milk, this meal proclaimed, then we would sup of the last like kings and queens.

It was too hot for such fare. The central cooling struggled, and power went out over dessert. My employer began a tirade against governmental restrictions on energy use. As we sat in the dark he promised the construction of a new solar grid that would end our reliance on Italy; he asked for funds to build it. *This is not an end*, he said, *but a new beginning.*

The lights came on over melted ice. Sour faces. Of the few questions asked about the solar grid, none were directed to the engineer at the table. ——— ——— — ——? said an Italian heiress. The diner across from her was more direct. He rubbed his fingers together in the universal question about money.

They are losing faith. My employer looked at me. *You have neglected your duties.*

It's the polar vortex that's at fault, Aida said. *They think it'll fix the smog for good. I heard the South Africans repeat a rumor about a farmer raising a new herd of Chianina. Fed with what grain, I ask?* She stepped close to me; for a moment, I thought she meant to grab my hand. *Don't forget, she's been taking care of herself. As you instructed.*

It is not your *job to mind her,* my employer said to his daughter.

Then give me a job, Aida said.

Can I trust you with it this time?

She straightened. *Yes.*

Impossible to imagine the man crying before his daughter over an absent wife. They had changed the day they put Eun-Young aside, honed to sharp new edges that snapped together.

My employer, declaring my weight satisfactory, ordered preparations for a harvest feast. It must showcase the country's abundance and put to bed any rumors of financial woes. *Ritualized celebrations in this season are historically successful in boosting tribal morale. We will need Kandinsky as our guest of honor. Do not fail this time.*

Aida, for once, had no clever retort. Even she treated the topic of Kandinsky with care. Residents now evoked his name with hushed reverence, attempting to scry from his business decisions the future of the planet. Was Kandinsky selling his stocks in global shipping companies, thus signaling that the world would grow more insular? Was he about to announce a new headquarters in California, indicating confidence in America's turnaround? Most importantly, would he invest in the country on the mountain?

Prepare your dogs, my employer said to Aida. *Kandinsky will enjoy a hunt. The British monarchy knew the value of this particular ritual in bleeding excess energy from their subjects.*

All two hundred and fifty-five residents were invited to the harvest. After the blow of the referendum results, the mood of our three-person planning committee was grim, single-minded, keyed up as if for battle. I'd find my employer seated in a dining room, scribbling so hard his pen gouged marks in the mahogany. Mostly numbers, scraps of words. *Circle the wagons*, I read on the bits that were in English. *Rally the troops.*

Make friends of enemies. It might have been funny had distress not hung in the air like oily smoke. Books accumulated: Sun Tzu's *The Art of War*, a dog-eared Italian edition of *How to Win Friends and Influence People*, *Utopia*, the reading list of a friendless teen boy that made me cringe. When my employer left to address a crisis with the new solar panels, I joked that there were more important things to do than plan a party. Aida said, gravely, *There is nothing more important.*

My employer insisted on a bonfire, against my faint protests. A construction crew descended to dig a roasting trench that split the lawn from end to end. Out of its coals the staff would lift theatrical mounds of potatoes and yams. A six-foot swordfish would grace the spit. I planned for my own duties to keep me far from the flames. I'd oversee salads dished out family style, rustic wooden spoons at the ready so that, along with saliva, guests might share goodwill and tender feelings. My employer added footraces and fire-leaping competitions with prizes of hundred-year port. He ordered the creation of two enormous communal tables of raw oak, each over a hundred meters long. No idea was too absurd, no expense too great. The simple bonfire grew into a wall of flames five stories high. *They will see a fire burning, unextinguishable, from the mountaintop.*

Our only real disagreement concerned the main course. I advocated for suckling pigs, roasted overnight.

No. You will have two hours, my employer said.

Woodfire cooking takes time. I can't perform miracles.

You will do it. Or I promise you, Eun-Young, I—

In the brittle silence, Aida stroked her father's arm. To me she said, *We'll use fresh meat from the hunt. It's better to sear it quickly, anyways.*

This news was a surprise to me. Not to my employer. As he strode from the room, I thought of the bird Aida's pups had caught in the spring. The hounds were so well trained that they had not broken the skin of their prey, not a feather. But they were no longer pups. Their teeth would be bigger.

It'll be fun, Aida whispered. *When you're hunting and the blood is up in you*— She trailed a finger up my thigh. *It's better than sex.*

Her father called from down the hall. She rolled her eyes but followed him, leaving me damp and furious.

As summer slanted and light grew dilute and the labs turned to plans for preservation, I noticed a new hardness that dropped around the two of them, as implacable as the steel doors belowground. Likely this wasn't new, and felt so only because I was present at those moments when we three became one and two.

They shared obscure references. Plans I wasn't privy to. I'd find them with heads tucked close as lovers', in arguments with the tepid flavor of meals reheated many times. *I have told you, Aida, the outrageous expense*— She, hissing, *I should just quit*—

But I knew she wouldn't. Oftener and oftener I thought of Aida's olive grove, the event she claimed had cut her and her father from the herd of common humanity.

I've heard it said that they were cruel, that the loss of the mother bled them of compassion. That they had no human feeling. It wasn't that. I've heard what they did called manipulation, brainwashing, a cult, but that wasn't quite it, either. Each resident had surveyed the menu of the wider world and chosen that mountain; name me one religious body, one government not steeped at the time in hypocrisy. While their constituents ate gray bread, members of parliament continued to accept fat bribes and fatter deliveries of Parmigiano, lamb's ears, truffles, as they deliberated policy that would determine the country's future. The secrecy Aida shared with her father was necessary—and, to them, pleasurable.

They had a fondness for dramatic reveals. The dinners, the rituals, the biblical references and rare ingredients, my employer waiting for silence before a toast, Aida reciting from memory the Latin names of each species in the lab, or Aida, in the dead of night, walking the edge of the cliff as she yelled into the wind that I should come look, that never again on all the earth would I see vistas as huge and clear and terrifying as these, the mountains and stars falling into the mouth of the night. She pointed her toes at the abyss. She turned walk into run into dance. This image lives on in the blazing silence of its night. It burned. It burns still. The older I grow the clearer I see it: how it does not want beauty: how it is itself. Primeval unsentimental thing throwing shadows on the walls of my memory. Feet pound this spot of earth. Knees and elbows jerk as if to tear free. I hear not wind but the drums and howls of a movement, not graceful, that seeks to escape the body's limits. Her stage is a starfield on which she pounds a rhythm into my chest: the thump, the ache. Again and again, that ache. And they say she had no human feeling. I don't know if it was human, but it was feeling. I felt.

I tried to pull her back. She evaded me, yowling with breathless laughter. *Eight years of lessons.* She cupped my cheek. *I promise you, I won't fall.*

She was so alive that night, opaline points in her eyes, mouth parted to bare her teeth. Ugly, and exquisite, and alive. I kissed her forehead for luck. I let her go.

I let her go.

Because what was the alternative to that dance they performed between madness and genius, between the back door and the olive grove that shimmered in the distance? I believed I'd seen the alternative in the world below, polluted and razed and overfarmed so that its dry soil held no secrets or mystery, no possibility of strawberries, Tasmanian tigers, cream. Sometimes, forgetting where I am and forgetting my age, I still wake in the night to the sound of my soul crying out in protest against leaving that country. I'd crawled on my knees through the ashes of my life to arrive at a world made possible by the vision of two people possessed of secrets, or narcissism, or lies, or wealth, or wisdom, or foresight, or bravery, or fear. Take your pick.

One afternoon, the sound of a phone jolted us from our harvest preparations. Aida lifted the device from her pocket. I expected my employer to reproach her for outside communications.

She held up the screen: *Roman*.

Father and daughter moved to a dining room. Upon their reemergence they looked at me in one movement, like those matched hounds. *Kandinsky will dine with us tonight*, he said, and she seethed with triumph.

Aida briefed me on Kandinsky's preferences as we ransacked the storeroom. Our guest had flown around the world keeping a scorecard of the restaurants at which he dined. He was a self-professed carnivore these days, scathing of meat cooked past rare. *Mildly ridiculous. Still, I ate extraordinarily well when I was his guest a few months ago.*

I thought you missed my cooking.

She didn't answer. Did I think mallard more appropriate, or moose? We took both. We bore fleshy bundles of venison, ptarmigan, water buffalo, sea eel, arctic hare up the damnable steps. Fearing this to be insufficient, Aida drove to the labs for cuts that dripped and wept. Cleavers unknit bone. Pressure cookers squealed out spumes of broth. Aida took charge of an ice cream. She was harried as I had never seen, her sweat tinny with fear. *He wants to make this deal*, she muttered to herself. *It must be perfect. If not—shut up, shut up,* — ———— ————. *We must impress him.*

Roman Kandinsky is now an urban legend, a bogeyman trotted out of the closet to frighten. His legacy has been ridiculed after a series of poor late-life investments, but at the time I met him, Kandinsky had just become the world's richest man. Even to the wealthy he was so wealthy as to be a different species. The country of Croatia was lifted from recession when Kandinsky took a liking to its beaches and built a vacation home, plus several manufacturing plants; certain historians pin America's downfall to a tax that chased Kandinsky's California business away. Moreover, Kandinsky boasted a blue-blood pedigree: the right schools, the right clubs, actual royals in the roots of his family tree. Because he'd built his first German company under an assumed identity, using public loans, people lost their shit at the aw-shucks, bootstraps story of prince to pauper to prince. They ate up his boyish flippancy. Kandinsky was photographed with politicians, actors, queens. What he had, in short, was the kind of clout my employer so desperately needed as the Italian government soured to the land of milk and honey.

Aida's excitement was infectious. I pictured a handsome stranger in a tailored suit, draped in the sash he wore in a photo with the king of Bhutan.

The man who came to dinner was blowsy, shuffling in sockless low-tops that exposed the ankles of an alcoholic. He was pushing forty but dressed like twenty-five, in sweatpants creased from his flight. Official photos were at least ten years out of date. The only evidence of the gourmand was a pair of flabby jowls. It was the work of a moment to imagine Kandinsky carved at the joints, his marbled flesh sizzling—an impression encouraged by the way Aida eyed him. She circled as if she were a mosquito and Kandinsky's blood life-giving. Even my impassive employer did his best to fawn.

Yooooo, Kandinsky crowed, slapping the doorway. *The famous Eun-Young. What's good.* A California vibe was part of his brand, as he liked to say in interviews, and he affected the swagger of the West Coast tech elite. *You're as hot as your daughter. No offense but, damn.*

Over bloody lamb he regaled us with tales of eating giant rat in the remnants of the Amazon rainforest. Over gazelle he spoke of hunting, with a Namibian minister, the last of the white rhinos. It was sheer flatulence, in response to which Aida put on a one-woman show of giggling and simpering and placing hand over heaving bosom like a Victorian debutante. I was too disgusted to eat. My employer barely touched his fork, so focused was he on anticipating Kandinsky's desires. He offered choice cuts to his guest. He suggested Kandinsky return after the birth of the new black rhinos, at which point the oldest bull could be spared. He described the harvest festival in such exaggerated terms that I touched my eyebrows to make sure they stayed in place.

If you resided here, naturally, my employer said, *you would not need an invitation to our festivities.*

I stared at the glossy center of my raw chop. Better that than the nakedness of my employer's want.

Of course, you are invited, dear Roman. Aida shone that night as a cut diamond does, all facets, all polished efficiency. *I'm allowed one guest at the harvest feast, aren't I, father? I might even let a very special one hunt with my own dogs.* Kandinsky asked about the prey. *It's a surprise,* Aida said, gleaming body angled toward her guest. *You know we'll provide what you can't hunt anywhere else.*

Yeah, okay, Kandinsky said, his gaze on her chest. *You always have the good stuff.*

After that it was swollen entendre after entendre until my eyes glazed over. At some point, with Kandinsky engaged by my employer, Aida prodded me. *Hey,* she said in a conspiratorial whisper. She struck the pose of an old-time starlet, hand to beleaguered forehead. *Hand me my Oscar, daahling, when this is over.*

Just the one?

What's that mean?

You've been playing this role for so long. So charming, so sophisticated. I looked down. *So good at picking shoes to hide your messed-up feet. Aren't you gunning for the lifetime performance award by now?*

Her lips went white. *Jealousy doesn't suit your complexion. You signed the contract, remember. You elected to take the role of mouse. I thought you were smarter than this. I thought you understood what we do here, what my father and I have sacrificed for. My father and I—we've given everything.*

She turned to Kandinsky, leaving me light-headed, trembling, as if I hadn't had enough to eat. Her hand remained on the table. I thought of yanking it into my lap. Thought of her damp with me, with a tiger's birthing fluid, grimy and true. She touched Kandinsky's arm, and I recalled her fear of failure, and my employer's disapproval, and where the limits of persuasion were drawn in his country in which capital was prized and lines blurred, blurred, blurred. For all Aida's declaration of seriousness and freedom, we both wore full-length cheongsams, traditional Chinese garments, often confused as Korean, tailored by

Western influence into dresses so tight that they hobbled the gait. Try to run and we wouldn't make it to the door.

I didn't take her hand. When called upon, I produced a fair imitation of Aida's public laugh: the little whinny, the acceptable feminine bray.

Over buffalo, my employer led Kandinsky into shoptalk. How many electric cars and ships Kandinsky had sold to which entities, his contract with China for moon tourism, his thoughts on the future of engineering and the likelihood that a breakthrough might still clear the smog. Kandinsky was surprisingly optimistic on this last point. *It's not the tech, man. I've got geniuses on my payroll that would give your daughter a run for her money. It's about interest. Branding. What's hot right now. Smog? Snore. Me, I'd rather—*

Aida kicked my ankle. We rose to fetch dessert.

Saavedra says you've got some pretty dope ideas, Kandinsky said as the door swung shut. *Rad that you bought his seeds and nuts. Never thought I'd see a man pay that much for another man's nuts.*

In the kitchen, Aida fumbled dessert spoons and could not locate the tureen. I refused to help. It was a long time before we drew on gloves and, unspeaking, took opposite ends of the serving tray. At the threshold of the dining room, Aida paused. I thought she meant to cut me down to size. Instead, she leaned over and kissed me. Not gently. Her teeth were in it, her tongue. I bit back. I forgot the guest on the other side of the door, the liquid nitrogen that hissed between us. I jammed my hip between her legs, eliciting a gasp she strangled to a whimper, a tender pink sound that invited breakage. I let go of the tray. I fisted her elegant bun. Her eyes went wide as I yanked up her tight skirt, *No*, she whispered, *don't rip it*— Pinned to the wall, she struggled, groin hot against my thigh, unable to extricate herself for fear of dropping the tray she now supported alone. Her arms trembled. Her eyes were slick, hateful. She ground against me in silence until she panted.

I helped her set the tray down. She was slow repinning her hair. I looked at the white stem of her neck, blood still thick in me; I wanted to bite it, break it. Guard it from prying eyes. Together we straightened the cheongsams she'd chosen with such care that I was surprised she'd extended this invitation. Only much later did I wonder if she'd been ordered to keep me till the men finished their talk.

Fresh blood ice cream, Aida announced as we entered. *With a special sauce.*

She upended the tureen. A black ribbon descended so slowly that it seemed a party trick; the liquid had already begun to clot. As the sauce steamed on contact with the ice, Kandinsky said, *Huh.*

This buddy of mine, he said, naming a tattooed chef I knew from the covers of glossy magazines. *He tells me blood with chocolate sauce is, like, a 2020 thing. The cacao washes out the flavor of the good shit.*

This isn't chocolate sauce. It's unadulterated snapping turtle blood, Aida said, and for the first time Kandinsky had no story of his own.

Like a waiting hunter, Aida moved in. Eyes on her stunned target, she began to speak of turtle blood and its legend of immortality. It was no legend I'd ever heard. For one, the underwater kingdom she described had a name suspiciously like Porsche. Tragic women featured alongside wise monkeys. *Ancient proverb*, she intoned to preface a plot twist ripped from the most absurd of our K-dramas, and I saw, if Kandinsky didn't, the wicked gleam in her eye. He was watching her arms flutter in the silk sleeves of that old-fashioned cheongsam, so unlike her usual style. It was, I understood at last, a costume. *Hers might be the shtick that wins him over*, the meteorologist had said of Aida's last visit to Kandinsky, meaning her education, her formidable mind; he'd been right, and wrong.

She avoided my gaze, thinking I'd judge her. I had. She flouted so many rules that I'd believed her free, by right of wealth and singular ferocity, from the stereotypes that trapped me. I wished she would glance my way so that I could say I forgave her—that there was nothing to forgive. But she had eyes only for her intended audience.

I knew there was a reason I came up here, Kandinsky said, swirling a finger in the turtle blood. *I've got advisors telling me to invest with the Swiss, or pick that colony in Patagonia—you've got enemies, man.* This to my employer. *They say your financials don't work out. Me, I trust my gut. Intuitive thinking's a big part of our corporate strategy. I lived in Japan for three months and learned about yin and yang, so when Aida came up talking about a philosophy of balance, and the species you've got hidden up here—well. Those dried-up sticks will die without tasting snapping turtle blood.*

Kandinsky raised his blood in a toast. The liquid slid over my tongue, warm and viscous as saliva. My employer's face grew serene as he drank. Aida sighed into her bowl, and Kandinsky threw his to the floor, where it shattered.

What is this shit? he screamed, pulling at his mouth, at nothing, at air—and then I saw the long, black hair. *Are you playing me? Everyone knows I choked on a hair at Kennedy's birthday. Are you trying to, like, assassinate me? Huh?*

As Aida turned to observe him, another strand slipped from her messy bun to trail, dark, against her neck. Kandinsky hadn't seen yet.

My employer had. His flat black gaze ticked between guest and daughter, one angrier by the moment, the other with her mouth curling into a small, contemptuous smile. Aida's lips parted. She was about to make some cutting comment. I saw my employer calculate the path to the most advantageous deal.

I threw myself at Kandinsky's feet, into that mess of blood and pottery. The seam of my skirt tore with a jagged hiccup. Ignoring the blood on my bare thighs, I prostrated myself—knees, chest, forehead, till my hair brushed shoe leather. Lips on the rug, I spoke.

——— ———— ——————————, ——————————— ———

———————————————— —— ————— ——— ——————————, I said, summoning the sound of hundreds of K-dramas.

Kandinsky kicked my hair away. Drew back with disgust. *What the fuck is she saying? You told me she's under some vow of silence. What kind of game is this?*

His fury, my employer's fury—I shut them out. I looked to the only person who understood, as I did, the game we'd laid out that night, and how we might play our remaining hand. Mischief dawned in her. Turning to the men, she said,

My mother is apologizing very deeply, from the bottom of her heart.

Many years later, I had the chance to meet the greatest actress of my generation. She proved insipid in her Q&A, that famous voice trailing so that more than one person asked her to speak up. Her face was symmetrical, pretty, a mannequin's. I thought myself old enough, by then, to know better, yet disappointment rankled. Then the actress left the stage. The lights switched off. The movie began and there she was: alive in full color. Performance, to paraphrase her wispy, nothing voice, is an alchemy possible only when shared. The night of Kandinsky's visit was the night I came alive as Eun-Young for the first, and last, time.

My face at his feet, Aida's raised and picture-pretty: together we were the complete performance of Kandinsky's desire. But beneath the contrition he saw, beneath the contempt my employer detected, a glimmering quicksilver current leapt, alive, between Aida and myself. As she glossed my faux-Korean gibberish, as we shaped language to do our bidding, I saw, beneath our supposed humility, the best of both of us: my ingenuity, her silver tongue, our magnificent bravado in daring to win a game in which we were seen as mere pieces.

———————— —— ———————— ———— ————

———— ———— ———————— ———— ————

——————.

My mother says she can no longer stay silent after dishonoring so great a man. She will perform acts of penance for her god.

———— ———— ———— ———— ———— ————.

My mother will fast for the next three days to cleanse herself.

———— ———— ———— —— —— ———— ————

————, ————————, ———— —— ———— ————.

Additionally, she will burn incense for our ancestors and visit the—the shrine, the family one, to ask their forgiveness and advice.

———— —— ———— ——, ———————— ————,

———— ———— ———————— ———— ————.

She is dreadfully sorry from the bottom of her heart. She hopes that so wise and generous a man can forgive her.

I looked up. Kandinsky was sitting back, nodding. He indicated that I should rise. I didn't dare look at Aida; I'd start laughing and never stop. There'd be time for laughter later, when we, stripped of costume, replayed this victory.

Cheerfully, casually, helping himself to Aida's half-drunk turtle blood, Kandinsky said, *But, like, how do I know she's sorry? I'm a visual learner. Seeing is believing.*

Between Aida and myself was blankness, confusion. But my employer comprehended. I heard static in my head, a false ringing, the end of language itself as my employer struck the first blow, backhanded, across my face.

There was no knock when, hours later, the door of my suite swung open to admit my employer. His gaze traveled dispassionately between me in the bed and Aida, who held ice to my swollen cheek. He announced that the deal with Kandinsky was done.

My employer gazed at a point just above my head as he named the size of Kandinsky's financial commitments and the critical equipment Kandinsky would manufacture in his German plants. He reported Kandinsky's timeline for moving to the mountain—the end of the year—and the key businesses that would follow Kandinsky into nearby Italian towns. He estimated the number of jobs Kandinsky would bring into Italy, and the points by which public approval would then swing in our direction. He named the friends Kandinsky had in parliament. *He plays golf with the president, if it comes to that.*

Aida shifted the ice to my other, marginally less painful, side. She congratulated her father.

It is the two of you I should thank. For the first time, I heard him praise his daughter. Her hand trembled on my cheek as he spoke of her persuasiveness, and of my skill in preparing meat to Kandinsky's taste. My employer finally met my eyes when he said, voice stranger than ever with emotion, *You behaved exactly as Eun-Young would have. You dem-*

onstrated unshakable faith in our mission. For this, you will forever have a place with us at the top of the list.

Us. As if, with a word, he could redraw a border that enclosed me on the safe side. He joined us at the bed, bending close; I thought he meant to kiss me. With disgust, with incredulity, and with a pity that has grown over the years, I saw that he truly believed us intimate. That we three were a twisted form of family. I jerked away.

Sorry, Aida said when we were alone. She dabbed the cut on my lip. *I'm so sorry, my heart. I swear I didn't know.* Yet she hadn't stopped the second blow, or the third. She'd apologized to Kandinsky, too. The air on the mountain was too thin, dispensing language into mere molecules. I made my words as solid as I could.

What is. The list.

It ranks every resident and staff member we'll bring along when we relocate. Moving off the mountain was always in the five-year plan. With Kandinsky's investments, we can proceed immediately. This is the best outcome we could have hoped for. We won't be left begging for Italy's scraps. After this move, we'll be out of their reach. We'll have a home to sustain us forever. Her voice was sweet with longing. Summer lay dying on the slopes. We we we we we to the throb of my cheek.

I'll sleep alone tonight, I said.

I still think about my turning Aida's sympathy away that night. Whether it later made a difference. I seized my small and jagged power to cut her, as if I might cut out, as well, the night's thick-clotted pain. I blamed her with a viciousness beyond what I felt toward the other two, as ugly-tender as a bruise. She alone had witnessed the moment in which I was stupid enough to think we'd won a game stacked against us, as if a lifetime lived under its rules had given me any kind of claim; and she'd seen Kandinsky rewrite those rules in a crude language of violence that made irrelevant our intelligence, our boldness, our love and need. That erased all that we were. I saw a new face to Aida on the night her father hit me, the face of a creature helpless and weak. A face that was my own. My own humiliation, doubled in her pleading eyes. I sent her away, to her father's house: I left her alone.

And so the milk ran dry. But first we had the luck of those creams, those spilled-down sauces, that summer of appetite that began with a soufflé cheesecake. There are very few ingredients to the recipe. Butter doesn't make the cake, nor cream. Its secret is ephemerality. Pull it from the oven and it is perfect; the next moment it is cooling, flattening, collapsing beneath the gravity of time. This is a flavor untasted by diners and critics, no record of its existence but for a private memory that lingers on one or two tongues. Aida of many faces. Despite all that came after, I put my palm to this summer that yields like warm dough and say, This is what it was like, this too is who we were.

Nine

✿

And so we come to the cusp of autumn, when summer breaks against the new season's chilly heart. I took two weeks off. My bruises faded. A raise arrived. My heart took a sick dip and soar at the zeros. I told Aida I was no longer angry, just recovering. I considered asking for painkillers but the thought of my employer approving the medication, monitoring my dosages and side effects, made me elect to self-medicate. So I drank. The oldest and most expensive bottles, 1992, 1980, 1893, rooms blurring till it seemed I could pass through time. Chewing hurt. I lost what little weight I'd regained. It didn't help that I stole two packs of cigarettes from the staff closet. I needed a reason to get up in the morning, and nicotine was the best I came up with. Puffing these solitary plumes, I imagined myself encircled by staff come to bitch about our shitty boss.

Lonely, I set the table for two and coaxed the cat to join me. Once I wadded Eun-Young's clothes in the back of the closet, he deigned to return to the bed that was once again peaceful, unbuffeted by sex. Some days we'd snooze till noon and I'd wake, cotton-mouthed, to his body so still that I wasn't sure he lived until I shifted and he stuck a claw in me. When he lay on my chest I did not, mercifully, dream of my employer, or Aida, or smog. The weight of the cat was an anchor dropped into deeper waters, stiller ones, and with him I drifted through dreams of crumbling sand beaches, of condensation down a bottle of Jarritos gulped roadside, and, most enduringly, of a dim kitchen in an apartment in Pasaje. Single window, covered plate. In the dream there was a chair pulled out, and steam rising from the dinner left out for me, and I woke just before the lid lifted with the green taste of something I could not name on my tongue. These were the nights the cat slept with me. In gratitude, I renewed my efforts to crack his appetite. I puréed calf livers, chicken hearts, mullet guts, the foulest enticements. For all my inventing, he lost weight, except for in his belly, which grew distended.

The nights got colder. The wind died down. The smog returned, thicker than before, puddling at the base of the mountain like bean soup. She was right. My resolve fractured. When Aida knocked again, my body reached toward the simple heat in hers.

We never spoke of the dinner with Kandinsky. We were gentler with one another, more careful, our lovemaking slower and drawn out to so exquisite a tension that I felt, on the cusp of pleasure, a sudden fragility that made me look away. In the chilly air I saw more clearly the cat's exhaustion, the smudges under Aida's eyes, the vulnerability in that brassy voice that mocked her father, that declared her out of reach of his approval. For the first time we were aware that what had knit us in the summer could, with the introduction of other allegiances, fray. Break. We never spoke of it. Instead Aida filled my ears with empty gossip about Kandinsky's preference for androgynous blondes, and I quit teasing her about her outfits, and she tolerated the cat. She even tried to train him. *Unchangeable,* she said with something approaching awe as he presented his ass to her face. *What* is *the point of him?*

She brought gifts from the residents. The South African mine own-
ers sent a card encrusted with semiprecious stones. *Tacky*, Aida said.
The English sheep heiresses sent a book of sudoku and a chunky shawl.
Maybe they think you're going senile. Bath salts, chocolates, an illustrated
guide of mobility exercises from which I gathered that the official reason for my absence was a twisted ankle. The concern, I knew, was not
for me, or even Eun-Young. It was for her husband, who controlled
the list.

The list. Oh, that list. Once I knew, I couldn't stop seeing it, the way
a horror movie leaves you spotting serial killers in every crowd.
Aida claimed she couldn't divulge, then caved and hinted. The list was
top secret. No one—except her, my employer, Kandinsky, and me—
could be certain of their placement. Length and composition shifted
from week to week based on variables Aida could not disclose. With
the move announced as two years away, residents grew anxious. Ten
people? I guessed, knowing how little patience Aida had for humanity.
Twenty? *About a hundred, plus support staff,* she finally said to shut me
up, and when I asked why not two hundred, why not everyone on the
mountain, she joked that only ninety-eight of a species were required
for breeding purposes if the world should end. *Speaking of breeding,*
she said, working a finger under my shirt, turning the conversation as
she turned my hips. After, I asked where. She waved vaguely. *Up.*

Remembering the meteorologist's predictions, I pictured the frozen
poles. Their blanked, icy grandeur. People had been saying Canada
was so deep in debt, so food-poor, that it would soon sell its northern
islands. These fantasies snowed over thoughts of the other list, for re-
entry to America, a concept that grew increasingly unlikely, abstract.

I began my own list based on observations of who'd laughed at or taken my employer's health advice, who'd invested steel or diamonds or capital. Each draft began with the balm of my name at the top. Aida joked that I should get a raise for every person I guessed right. At least I think it was a joke. I looked forward to finalizing my predictions at the harvest feast.

Kandinsky sent his RSVP, Aida told me.

Cool as she tried to play it, her body betrayed her excitement. We were baking. I pounded semolina more ferociously. A mill would have been quicker, but my employer required the rustic texture of ancient loaves. And so I followed recipes from the sixteenth and nineteenth centuries despite the fact that heritage grains were never my heritage. Autumn was a harvest of big-box stores and their back-to-school sales: fruit leather, instant mac 'n' cheese, and bread that we unhusked, crinkling, from its plastic sleeve. My mouth watered for the sweetness of processed wheat sown thick through gas stations from California to New York. Honey Buns and Wonder Breads, in perfect squares and machined circles, and the ripe weight of a Danish, mass-produced, that attempts no fidelity to the country after which it is named—no country but this one ambered by waves of industrial grain. I felt a cut in my soul like the vent through which steam escapes in baking.

Aida was telling me not to worry about the hunt. She'd positioned me and Kandinsky on opposite sides of the field. I wouldn't even see him.

Where's your position? I asked, though I knew before she spoke his name. She had an explanation for this, academic in its precision. I cut her off. *Don't worry about me. I won't hunt.*

Our guests will expect it.

They'll expect me in the kitchen, cooking.

———

I was at the stove when the hunt began. Through the glass the moon was a ripe blood orange, each star skewering through. I saw the meteorologist's hand in the composition, his value on the rise as weather grew overcast and he was called upon to clear the sky. Aida spoke of him with a taunting yet proprietary tone, as if of another dog to train.

The lawn seethed with hunters. In that sea of red jackets, Aida stood out in green tweed. Her overcoat belled out from the waist and swept over her horse's hindquarters, the fusty fabric cut to be as modern and dramatic as a rocket ship. It flared as she trotted down the line to her position beside Kandinsky. I would have been with those on foot, far behind; I didn't ride.

The hunting call, when it came, seemed to ring from the mountain itself, as if solid rock had become the clapper of an enormous bell. The sound pealed from all directions at once, eerie and sourceless, so that the dogs whined in dismay. Though I knew of the two hundred and fifty speakers planted in the ground, I shivered. It was a mix of whale song and passenger pigeon cry: the sound of extinction.

The prey appeared far down the slope in silhouette. They were meant to be a secret until the last possible moment. I glimpsed dog-sized creatures that ran with awkward, shambling gaits. One reared on its hind legs, disquieting. I returned my gaze to the inert meat on my cutting board. When I looked up, both hunters and hunted were gone.

I served mulled wine to the motley dozen who remained. Most were very young or very old, and their faces, unusual in a country of specimens at their prime, lent the gathering a familial air. Wood smoke, hot drinks, the swordfish crisping over flame: a portrait of abundance. I took generous tastes and signaled the staff for less juice, more wine, more brandy.

I would give half my fortune to be seventeen once more, said the older English sheep heiress. She'd seized this minor stage to reminisce on family fox hunts. *I have had doubts about our host, but let it be said that he is a champion of traditions.*

They outlawed hunts for animal cruelty, didn't they? said the Iranian meteorologist from his side of the circle.

We go too far when animal rights are upheld over human ones. The heiress lifted her chin. *It was another form of cruelty to destroy a cornerstone of our heritage. Though it is not said often enough these days, my culture should not be passed over. There is no shame in honoring an empire that contributed across centuries and continents.*

One investigator found forty-three lacerations on a single vixen, the meteorologist said. *I'm finding it hard to understand the point of that savagery.*

An Italian automaker made *tsk*ing sounds as he rubbed the sprained ankle that had kept him from the hunt. *Sopravvivenza*, he said, meaning survival, another of my employer's terms that I had come to recognize. He sided with the heiress. The son of a French director took the meteorologist's part. Others chimed in, the debate affable and evenly matched until the young daughter of a British tech founder piped up. The group quieted to admit that halting, childish voice, the heiress smiling encouragement until the girl arrived at her point: she, personally, was okay without that part of British heritage. The pro-hunting contingent was at a loss. The meteorologist high-fived the girl, and the two of them began to awkwardly negotiate a sequence of fist bumps.

Don't touch her! The British heiress thrust a spindly arm over the girl, who stumbled, surprised, and fell. The heiress didn't appear to notice. Her thin nostrils flared at the meteorologist, as if taking in his scent. *How dare you speak of savagery given what your people do to innocent women and girls.*

The fire popped. Cracked. I rose to stir it, putting myself between heiress and meteorologist. Employing the oldest trick in the hosting book, I topped off the old woman's glass. Liquid trembled over the rim. I mimed an apology, handed her a napkin, dabbed her arm, coaxed her to a dry patch where I ministered to nonexistent splashes on her skirt. The meteorologist got up. *Et tu, Brute?* he muttered as he passed me.

The heiress limited subsequent nostalgia to the fashions and foods of old, but through the gap in the circle cold air came in. Faces formed crude woodcuts in the leaping flames. I recalled an earlier version of myself who'd floated a petition against cage-raised chickens, and imagined her staring from the meteorologist's vacated spot. I signaled frantically for more drinks.

I left the swordfish to the staff and snuck to my usual smoking spot, where I met the unpleasant surprise of my employer.

I stopped with my lighter in my hand. My employer's face was vivid orange in the fire's glow. We hadn't been alone together since that private dinner with Kandinsky. In front of diners I could pretend nothing had changed; I slipped into Eun-Young's role as easily I did her silks, which no longer stank to my desensitized nose of her perfume. Alone with my employer, I was at a loss.

I didn't dare light my cigarette, and I was too stubborn to toss it. I kept hold as I asked why my employer wasn't hunting.

I don't ride. The hounds bellowed downslope, echoed by a human roar. He said, with yearning, *Though I was tempted.*

Apex predators shouldn't be seen traveling on foot with the rest of us. *Right.* My tone was sharper than intended. I'd sampled quite a bit of mulled wine.

It is one of many skills a person must acquire young to perform convincingly. I did not grow up with my daughter's privileges.

How'd you grow up?

It was a bid to flush him from my smoking spot; I expected his usual retreat when faced with pointed inquiries about his origins. To my surprise, he described an island off the eastern coast of Italy famous for its seafood. Every year the local Romani population, still called "gypsies" by many, lit harvest fires. I thumbed my cigarette and grew ever more bitter as my employer spoke of crystal water and yachts, illusions as pretty as his voice on the phone, as Eun-Young. I should have played along. But I touched a sore spot inside my cheek, the last bit of the harm he'd done me, the harm I'd let him do, the harm I'd been paid to let him do. I could hold back neither a burp nor my disdain.

How very fucking nice for you. Want my advice? Add a sprinkle of white sand and beluga caviar to that story to really dazzle your guests.

I turned to go. He grabbed my arm.

It was not nice. The fires stank of seaweed and fish guts. I was made by my father to hawk shells to tourists so that we might buy grain.

He released me, smiling with no feeling in the eyes, and I saw: there was no body behind the mask. His was the demeanor of a person forced to grow up servile, until the mask became he. The absolute nothing of it chilled me more than a display of power.

If you deem the raise for your occupational injuries insufficient, I am open to negotiation. I do not discount your value. You understand that a display of humility is one valid strategy for survival. We are more alike than you think.

I've got enough blood money, I spat.

I lit my cigarette. The first drag passed a cool breeze over my body. I waited to see if I would tell him to fuck off, to deny any similarity between us, to say that what had happened with Kandinsky must never happen again. To say: *I quit.*

I took another drag.

At the crucial moment, my daughter was too proud to see the necessary adaptation. You were quick to realize that men like Kandinsky require a bit of groveling. I raised my daughter to rise above the position I was born to. Perhaps she grows too bold. Senior staff complain about her dismissal of the chief zoologist. That man was not easy to woo to our cause, and I suspect he will not be so easily gotten rid of. My daughter tells me I worry too much, that budgets are just made-up numbers. He was incredulous, and bitter, yet I heard, too, pride. *Tell me. Was the zoologist angry?*

The man had not wilted before Aida, as others did. He had meant to match her. *Furious.*

She forgets that it is the group, not the individual, that ensures the continuation of a species.

When I remember this night, knowing what I do now, I pity the strange, cold man who paid me. Perhaps he doesn't deserve it. But I have a daughter now. I remember the day she looked at me with the face of a stranger and I saw in her an ability to walk where I could not follow, into worlds she would prefer to mine. On that night, dressed in Eun-Young's clothes, I believed the ghostly touch was that of the missing woman, not my own self reaching through time. On that night

I felt mean. *So what if Aida thinks she knows everything. Who didn't when they were twenty? In any case, it's a little late to fix a lifetime of bad parenting.*

My wife believed so.

My mother's face rose up. I said, *She shouldn't have given up. What kind of mother does that?* A pricking where Eun-Young's wool coat touched my skin, a chafing. *What's the worst Aida can do?*

Keep her close. Using whatever methods you must. My face grew hot under my employer's knowing gaze. *It is good that she has you to remind her of humility. As I have my staff.*

I took a beat to understand. Few traces, after all, remained of the boy from the fishing isle. I raised a hand to my employer's jaw. The orange makeup rubbed off, his skin beneath browner, tougher, weathered by sea. He leaned into my touch. As the bonfire blew the scent of fish and smoke, I asked how many staff members originated from his island.

The majority of them, now that the island has flooded. Low country, you see. It was almost a joke. But when I asked how many staff would join us in our move, he lost his lightness. *Fewer than I might like. My daughter remains conservative with calculations for her list.*

What do you mean, her *list?*

He looked at me. I was the one to look away.

Will you wonder about the ones you leave behind? I asked.

After Eun-Young, I learned that it is best not to dwell. Take only what is essential from the old life and move forward into the new. That is survival. I asked if this worked. *I am wealthy. My daughter has grown into her potential. The island continues in a form, and I have built around me my own tribe, stronger than any other, with the qualities necessary to prevail under any conditions. I have you.* I was oddly flattered until he said, *Still, I wonder. Why is it that you are, on paper, perfectly adequate—yet I find you not nearly as appealing as my first wife?*

He ceased in that moment to be frightening, violent, ridiculous, unknowable. His sorrow had an awful gravity. We stood together and smelled, beneath the smoke and fish, the lingering sweetness of dying sedge. At least, I smelled it. I didn't ask if my employer could. I didn't ask how long it would take to stop smelling Eun-Young's grass, as I had stopped smelling her perfume. How long to erase all traces of a person. I was occupied with this question when my employer plucked the cigarette from my lips.

If the embers burned him when he closed his fist, he gave no sign. *Your health is no longer yours to despoil*, he said as he touched my stomach beneath my coat. I waited for his hand to move as the hands of men do, my body going passive in that instinctive female way so as to smooth his passage, get faster to the after. He stopped at the prominence of my hip, unprotected by fat or muscle. He bore down into bone. A nauseous line of pressure carved through me. *Take care. Your body mass index has fallen below seventeen. Eighteen to nineteen is ideal for a long, fertile life.*

I was dangerously close to sober as I approached the bowls of mulled wine. Empty. I hoisted one in my arms. The voices of dogs gnashed at the night. *Our intrepid hunters return!* cried the heiress. I opened the restaurant door. A black streak shot past me, escaping downslope. The cat.

I could not make myself understood. Could not. I sketched whiskers and ears in the air, pawed at nothing. The tech founder's young daughter regarded me with concern, but others mimed back, thinking me entertainment. I sprinted away to applause. I called for the cat. The hounds called louder, keening their bloodlust and need.

I crashed into the meteorologist. *Cat*, I gasped, mindful even then of my ruse. I aped the accent of a nonnative speaker. *Gone. Cat. MY CAT.* He set down his notebook; he'd been sketching a tree. *I'll help*, he said as the hunting party came over the rise. I ran into that wall of hooves.

STOP, Aida said. Then she was dropping from her saddle, holding me close. *My cat*, I wheezed into her shoulder so that the riders would not hear. Kandinsky's face floated behind her. *He escaped. I'm worried about the dogs. What if they—* Into that voice I loved came a note of relief, so that I sagged before I caught the words. *And here I thought you had some kind of emergency. He'll be fine.* She took her reins back from Kandinsky. The riders went on to the party.

My employer draped his arm over me. *Don't keep our guests waiting.* I heard the heiress proclaim that when she was young, she and her husband— He released me at the fire with a shove. Half a dozen staff were hoisting the swordfish from the spit. It had my employer's sunken black eye and I choked with panicked hilarity. In the flickering light the staff had his same build, his weathered skin. I backed away from them and swiped a glass from a tray. Real wine now, undiluted. Eun-Young's name was yelled. I pulled my shawl over my head. Every shadow could have been a black cat. Every shadow and its licked flame could have been my black cat, torn and red and bleeding. I saw him die a hundred deaths.

I was found. I batted well-wishers away. Aida appeared cradling a bottle and I nearly wept with gratitude. *Not for you, you lush. Get ahold of yourself.* She emptied the liquor into a tub at the fire's edge. Plucked birds swam within. Larger animals turned on a spit. The smell of singed hair—

When I looked into the flames it was with a sense of calm, as if I had already lived this night, and I recognized, as you recognize the smell of your own breath and the face of your father as a child and the touch of a lover you have only just met, the bodies that undulated in a red-gold torrent of flame without end. All those arms and legs. The black stars of those curled fingers. In the fire I saw the face of my mother shrunken to a dead black mask. I lifted my hand to hers.

Aida yanked me back. My cuff was smoking.

Somebody's starving, she said.

Laughter.

Many open mouths.

It was not my mother's face. Still, I watched it burn.

Nor was it a human face, though I could be forgiven my confusion. My employer delivered a speech in several languages as staff pulled the main course from the flames. In each tongue I heard, *Pan troglodytes aurum*, the Latin name for the prized golden chimp. This was the last band of the species on earth, brought back from the brink of extinction. My employer named each resident whose investment had made the project possible. He raised a toast. Once, millions of years ago, chimps and humans had split from the same genetic line; these were our closest living relatives. Yet only one of our two species remained. Aida, beside me, mouthed the words along with him. Winter was at our doorstep and numbers did not lie. It was time to put exploration aside for efficiency. Golden chimps were one of several species the labs had deemed insufficiently hardy, useful, or nutritious enough to take in our move. Space and labor were better spent elsewhere. We should not see this as failure, but as a lesson in perseverance. The chimps had lost; we triumphed.

This harvest had propelled us into a state of complete self-sufficiency, such that everything eaten and drunk would, now and forever, come from the mountain, for the mountain. We were to celebrate that.

A ritual:

One by one the residents approach the two laden tables. Some take a breast of quail, some a spoonful of mushrooms, some the jewel-bright Japanese yams renowned for their high concentrations of vitamin A and copper. There is hesitation around the table that holds the main course. Staff members have removed the heads but still the comparison to a human body, a small human body, say the body of a child, is undeniable. There is also the question of serving size. To eat you must reach up and crack a shin from a thigh, pull a rib from its partner. Kandinsky is the first. He grasps the charred flesh in both hands, and when it parts, when it gives way to the blood-red, jellied interior, he whoops. He whirls a forearm above his head like a boy with a fairground prize. *They promised the rarest meat on earth. Fuck me if this isn't cooked to perfection.*

After that the spell is broken. Guests choose a seat at one of the two long tables. There are those who fill up on squash and rice, those who only drink. Those whose faces show aghast in the chiaroscuro light. Aida leads me to the table heaped with limbs. She stacks my plate. Beyond the tangle of meat I catch my employer's eyes glinting like those of a beast on open savannah. He notes my plate. He notes every plate. He stands as if painted or sculpted against the night, dark Anubis weighing wallets and hearts. How many observe the way his eyes flick to his daughter, who from time to time nods or shakes her head?

I didn't taste the chimp. Ask where is the line, why it was drawn—I can't say, but I didn't taste. My employer spoke of us as united, a great family having found one another across the wastelands. He referenced the forty years the Israelites wandered the desert, and then, pausing for his punchline: *Though they'd have gotten to their destination faster if they had our funding.*

Good riddance, Aida said, nodding at the older sheep heiress who, despite her grandstanding about hunts, had chosen the table of vegetables. A line cook sat beside her. The staff had been given time to change before joining the feast, and as the cook split parsnips, I saw the glitter of a cufflink from my employer's collection. *I'd take even fewer people if it were up to me*, Aida murmured. *But my father isn't as lucky as we are. He still needs others.*

It dawned on me that I was looking at a version of the list made flesh. The night was no game. *Apice*, diners said to the clink of glasses. This was survival of the hungriest.

Your meat's going cold. My father won't think well of waste. She tipped my chimp onto her plate.

Like a ghost I floated with an after-dinner tray. I was transparent with hunger, yet every dish stank of burned hair. Those guests named in my employer's speech were glassy-eyed with an ebullience I associated with junkies about to get their fix. Others were silent, or horrified, or bitter. They discussed alternative communities in Tibet, Ontario, Hawaii. *Air quality is excellent, but the tax rates!* Antarctica, New Zealand. ————————*cryogenic*————. A woman with lipstick on her teeth spoke shrilly of an underwater city being constructed in the Mariana Trench, only twenty million euros per plot for the first hundred investors. Still others evoked the names of scientists who claimed that conditions would improve, that the smog—

I ferried empty trays into the kitchen. I washed a half-eaten cheese-board and looked up at the red wound of the moon. My hands swam in the sink among discards. Guts and bones, tail and scale. All the wine came up at once, elemental and sour, and when hollow I crammed myself with half-gnawed cores and hard ends of Gruyère, with scrapings of quince that squelched beneath my nails. This ballast kept me anchored as I saw the guests off, dispensing to each a sachet of breakfast granola, so that they might wake up well-fed the next day.

Aida came to bed barefoot, full of easy consolation. *Relax, the cat will turn up. Come, come.* She massaged my shoulders as she described the sight of her work brought to fruition. The pack had obeyed its training: not a single chimp was injured when the dogs held them down with soft mouths. *Beautiful*, she said. I pictured a red flood pouring downslope. Not only were the dogs harmless, Aida assured me, but electric fences had been established at the border following the arson attempt. Animals could detect the fence. The cat would not escape. *You're overreacting, love. All will be well.*

That night I looked into the shadows of the room and saw dead things clotting and said, *You know everything, don't you. About me, the cat. What should live or die.*

I was waiting for you to climb this soapbox.

I shook her hands off. *This wasn't a spare peacock or a piece of rotting mammoth, Aida. You hunted a species to extinction.*

Thanks, but even my dogs aren't that good. A few got away.

I didn't laugh. *I thought chimps were charismatic megafauna. Now they're prebi—preliba—delicacies? Who decided?*

Kandinsky expected something one of a kind. This loss is more than balanced out by what we gain from his investment. With his money, we'll fund research that ensures the continuation of a half-dozen keystone species without which entire ecosystems would collapse. For many minutes she spoke the language of calculation. Only once did she say, *Regrettable.* I thought of her cupping a chimp's golden cheek in the sanctity of the lab, but before I formed my question she said, *My point is, the chimps were poised for extinction before we bred them. This would have happened anyway.*

Not in this way.

She slid from bed and bowed. *Would Madame care to hear the specials?* Moonlight aproned her thighs in white. Her face was the image of courtesy as she offered an imaginary menu. *How do you prefer your extinction served tonight? Low fertility à la DDT? Broiled with a side of wildfire and climate change? My methods are cleaner.* The chimps, shot with anesthetic darts, had died instantly, free of suffering. Her logic landed with sickening blows. I put hands to my ears.

I'm getting sick of your pious act, she said.

It's what I'm paid for.

Please. As if you never ate tuna, or used plastics, or flew on planes when gas was artificially cheap. Every person on this planet had a hand in killing the chimps. We must be equally responsible for the tough calls, and I will do the job if no one else steps up. At least I gave the chimps a chance. Only think—it was the grandest of exits. They won't be forgotten after tonight. Not a part of them went to waste. Wouldn't you choose to go out with a bang and not a whimper?

That's insane, I said.

What's insane is the idea that I should fix what I didn't break.

If you're trying to abdicate responsibility for what happened tonight—

Oh, no. I admit to blood on my hands. She waggled them. Her nails were pearly, clean. *If you insist on getting all moral about it, the Abrahamic god did plenty of smiting.*

I couldn't speak for a minute. *I knew you were full of yourself. I didn't think you had an actual god complex.*

She smiled. *If I were omnipotent, I'd do a much better job than whoever's pulling the strings. I'd re-create the birds and the beasts, the skies and the waters, greater biodiversity, clean air, no industrial farms. Believe me, I fantasize more than anyone about a world in which I don't have to make these decisions.* She turned her hands over and over in her lap. *In that world, I'd have time to do something utterly frivolous, like dance. That was my mother's plan for me. She wanted another artist in the family. She sang. But . . .*

Weeks after losing time in the olives, Aida had come down with the flu. She lay in bed watching daytime news. It was the summer the bees died. *Remember?* How could I forget. During lulls in coverage of bombings and protests and market crashes, networks played B-roll of empty aviaries and dripping comb. Black bodies buzzed at Aida's vision as her fever spiked. The bees ceased to haunt her the day she came across an interview with an esteemed American technologist. *Brand said, "We are as gods and have to get good at it." That was it—no clouds parting, no messenger dove for me.* Self-mockery vanished as Aida said, *I heard, loud and clear, what I am needed for. My father was the first person to take me seriously.*

She must have been eleven or twelve. *He made you do this?*

I chose, she said with cold fury. *Me.*

You chose these *people as your apex predators?* I saw her wince at the word. *I can't believe it. I won't. You hate them. You don't care how well they eat.*

You miss the point, as usual. It's like asking if I love or hate a particular milkweed plant, an individual partridge. This isn't a matter of personal sentiment. Apex predators have their role in the ecosystem. Saber-tooths thinned herds, too. When I pressed, she said, flatly, *It's creepy how you begin to sound like her. She went irrational at the end. She was perfectly happy to give to churches built by human hands, but GMO corn, that was unnatural. I asked her, what kind of god kills the bees and leaves rapists alive? Not one I can respect.*

We were quiet.

If I were omnipotent, I said, sadly, *I'd choose the world in which you can dance.*

With a shrug, she promised to dance down the mountain in the morning. *Naked, with tassels on my tits if that'll stop your moping. Don't you see that dance is inconsequential compared to what I do now? I used to waste hours moving a wrist or a toe. Who needs* that *when the world is burning?*

I never asked about need. Don't you want to give it a real go? Onstage?

No.

I wanted to shake her, she was so stubborn. *You must have. At least once.*

To my surprise, she asked if I knew the Gehry performance hall in Los Angeles. I did. Though I'd never been inside, the building spoke to me across downtown's dull, linear drone. Its curved panels billowed as if to catch the wind of another world.

That's the one. We used to talk about having my dance debut there. Pravat's Fire Bird *and a costume my mother had all planned out. Red sequins, if I remember.* Aida looked at herself in the window as if she might glimpse that glitter even now. She smiled, twelve again. Then her face slammed shut. Time made its brutal passage. *It was a tacky outfit for a mediocre performer. I didn't have the right lines, the hips—I'm not made for dance. The Gehry was a pipe dream and anyhow, it closed, which proves my point. Who cares about dance? I care about sustainable crops. I care about red winter wheat because of its high yield. I care about Tasmanian tigers for their insights on genetic drift in an isolated environment, plus I'm a sucker for Calvin and Hobbes. Well, Hobbes.* "Poor, nasty, brutish, and short." *He was right about life for most people, but not for us.*

She touched me then, not as a waiter, not as a dancer or a young god, but as Aida. Her hands were soft and they knew me. *I was made to do* this. *Trust me, okay? Because I care about you.* She kissed my palm, taking into her mouth my unwashed fingers. *See? I don't complain when your hands get dirty.*

That wild laugh of hers. It was a child's laugh forced out of a woman-girl who should have learned, by now, to tame it; but that child was trapped at the moment in which she set aside mother and made her promise to father. Revulsion moved through me at that unnatural sound. I could not bear it. Could not. I put my hand to her mouth and her laugh spilled through lips and teeth. I wanted to stop her; I wanted it to stop.

Aida reeled back, gasping. The moon slid distant and unbothered across the sky, red as the imprint of my fingers on her throat. Beyond it a million billion movements of other bodies invisible to us, though who was to say we didn't feel their tug at our lives, move in thrall to their gravity? *Yes,* she said, following my gaze. *Just like that.* I pulled sounds from the depths of her, not cool, not aloof, but low, earthy. Here. As we fell asleep, she murmured, *So you do understand.* I asked what she meant. Into my nape, gentle as a lamb, she said, *To want to kill is to want to live.*

Dawn brought to the restaurant a lab tech, who bore in his carrier one squalling, spitting cat. The tech mumbled and wouldn't meet my gaze—embarrassed, I thought, by the smell of sex in the air, or the cat's utter disinterest in me.

You should get some medicine on those scratches, Aida said as I tussled with the cat. I was trying to take his pulse. She studied him as she had the chimp in the lab, head cocked, assessing. *I need to talk to you about him.*

I got my hand on his chest. His small heart buzzed but I couldn't judge its speed; my own was racing, too. *He stays*, I said. *I don't care how irrational I'm being. If he goes, I can't—please*, I said to the raging parcel of fur and bone, unable to keep the anger from my voice. *Please, please, just listen to me.*

His eyes pulsed yellow. He settled a fraction. I scooped him up.

I'd never ask that of you, Aida said. *Never.*

But last night—

She had sent out a search party, she said, the moment she dismounted. She hadn't wanted to get my hopes up; she'd meant to surprise me. She wasn't cruel, and this was not the only time I misjudged her. I closed my clumsy mouth. I put my free hand, the one not holding the cat, in hers.

I know what he is to you, she said.

A goddamn pest.

Family.

She took him from me. His pupils narrowed, I was ready to call out a warning—and then he, recalcitrant beast, closed his eyes against her arm. She didn't protest his matted fur, or the saliva that he, of late, oozed onto every surface. He was a threadbare thing and yet his purr, as it passed between us, knit, in its low harmony, all our other snags. As three we were unexpectedly whole, a different grouping of three that I think about to this day. For all the miracles I witnessed in that country, this may have been the greatest.

Aida offered a full veterinary checkup at the lab, which I declined. There wasn't a scratch on the cat, and I'd fallen behind with dinner prep. But late that afternoon, in the pause between mis-en-place and service, I made myself look at the cat, really look, the way Aida had, frank and unsentimental. I observed the limbs that draped and flexed, predatorial in the just-dusk light. The ears that spun like satellites, a beauty of attunement in cartilage and vein. And I saw how his fur, now thinned, stretched over bones I could count when he took a breath. I changed my mind.

I left the restaurant holding the cat and a warm tarte tatin, intending to drive to the lab. The car sat where I'd parked it on my first day. The door, dusty, was still unlocked. But the engine would not start. The fuel gauge read empty, though I hadn't drained it.

I lay my gift to the side and tried to remember the language of my new contract, the sole copy of which my employer had taken with him. I could leave restaurant grounds; how was not specified. As the tart cooled, I wondered if I could have located the lab had I driven there. If I could have passed through that hatch, or any other, or the border fence. The lab assistants had been forbidden visits to family, the Iranian meteorologist given a poisoned gift of dates. I thought of telling Aida that while saber-tooths may have killed and eaten aurochs, they did not herd, or fatten, or force their prey into strange clothes. Her father's definition of apex was not hers. When the tart grew cold, I went back in.

The phone was ringing.

I intended to rebuke you for last night's behavior, my employer said.

However. The emotion I'd displayed for the missing cat had persuaded a few desirable holdouts, residents who trusted the science of the country but not the intentions behind it. Such investors wanted to move to a place where tender feelings prevailed. They were willing to pay for it. *Well done.*

Two nights later, I heard Eun-Young singing in my dreams. She sat at a piano in the center of the kitchen and played a hymn, pensive and crashing with the thunder of the old gods. Her voice was an anvil. Impossible that it should emerge from so slight a body. It made a listener believe, if momentarily, in some high, pitiless power. The kitchen floor crumbled beneath her bit by bit. The song continued when I woke. I followed it out of the restaurant. Against the glass lay a single, undersized chimp. Breath whistled in its mouth—that was the sound I'd heard. Bones moved broken in its chest. Its cheek, a bloody crater. I didn't know if I should keep it cool and dry, wash it with a warm cloth, feed it sugar and honey, grubs and flies. In the end, I carried the chimp on my hip—it was small, a juvenile—and I walked, *psst*ing occasionally, through the restaurant. I hummed the tune from my dream, which morphed, as dream-things do, and became a tune my mother had picked out from deep in the pit of her labor, a patriotic march from the ruinous childhood during which she and her siblings had, to fend off starvation one winter, hunted and killed and eaten the neighbor's fluffy white dog. As a child I'd believed this to be a horror story, and feared my mother as consequence. Now I wasn't so sure. To survive: to eat. When I found the cat, I set the dying chimp before his lamp-green eyes. *So live*, I said, and as he sniffed, it seemed I could taste the blood on my own lips, my own tongue.

Ten

❋

I t was in October, after the lawn had been raked of ashes, after the
grass had succumbed to first frost, that I felt the constriction of
possibility. What had seemed expansive, Edenic, took on the air
of an amusement park right before close. The age of exploration was
over. Unwanted guests were to be escorted out. One afternoon, Aida
asked if I wanted to see something incredible. *Once in a lifetime.* We
drove to the breeding lab. The hatch was flung wide, scientists tromp-
ing through mud. A great buzz rose from the churned ground.

Cicadas, Aida said of the million eyes that glittered from their cage.
*This species emerges from its larval stage once every thirteen years. I planned
to study the biochemistry of their stasis, but we've run out of time.*

So?

So I thought, rather than euthanize them, why not let them fly once.

She waited, then stalked off, upset at my ingratitude. I stood with
hands jammed into my pockets as cicadas took to the sky in a cloud that
flashed sienna and umber and the deep, red-brown of old oaks. The
sound was shattering, enormous. If I listened hard it seemed that I
heard snatches of pattern, rhythm, melody—that if I listened long

enough, I might hear a whole symphony. But we didn't have that time before the swarm flowed downslope.

Belatedly, I remembered secrecy. Wouldn't a cloud of extinct insects rouse suspicion?

Most will die when they hit the electric fence, Aida said. *Any that fly high enough to pass over are unlikely to last more than a day in this cold.*

And if they do?

Not my concern. She shrugged one pale shoulder; it was as if she'd rammed it into my chest. *They can fend for themselves if they get so lucky. As for us, my father will take care of any political fallout.*

I began the long walk back to the restaurant, unable to watch the cicadas meet electricity. Aida picked me up from the side of the road an hour later, her jaw tight as she spoke into the phone. Her father's voice rumbled through silicon. I later heard that the cicadas that escaped were mistaken for a swarm of locusts. People fell to the ground and prayed, believing this to be the end of the world.

The thinning of unwanted residents was only a little less brutal. In November, thirty families were told they had failed to make the list. Few were gracious about it. An Italian munitions dealer smashed the windows of his house before leaving. An Austrian trader attempted to steal a clutch of peregrine falcon eggs. Shelves began to empty in the storeroom, and though meals remained lavish, nutritious, decisions were made. Koshihikari rice over Carolina Gold, blood oranges over Seville sours, the younger British sheep heiress over the older, infirm one. *At least we'll never have to deal with cilantro or black licorice again*, I said to the sleeping cat.

One night, I uncapped a bottle of whiskey only to be hit by the mean smell of piss: a rejected resident's last, inventive fuck-you. My eyes watered but, really, it was no worse than Roquefort or natto. I took a greedy sniff. I'd once spent a layover with a friend who lived six roommates deep in a rambling San Francisco Victorian that squatted on the seam between the gentrified and seedy sides of town. Leaving the house early on Sunday morning, I smelled, from one corner, the stale urine of Saturday's barflies; and from the other, fresh loaves turned out by an exquisite French bakery. The thrill was in both. I described for Aida the house: the perpetual pot of vegan soup that scented the bedrooms with tumeric, the roommate who made mosaics from broken glass. Her face contorted. *Why the fuck did you keep it?* She called staff to dispose of the urine.

I slept fitfully, the ammonia a sharp reminder of places off the mountain.

I tuned in to gossip about communities in New Zealand and Croatia. One resident destined not to make the list spoke with longing of a family farm in Vermont, another of an ashram in Kerala. The government there had committed to investments in air quality. I used to frequent a grubby takeout joint, Raj or Sultan's something, where the Malayali cooks stubbornly made, in addition to chicken tikkas and garlic naans, their own region's lacy, rice-flour bread. I waited for the conversation to come around to appam, but it never did.

The chill in the air unlocked a primal code in me. The wind blew hard, and had grit in it. Stepping outside, I felt again my terrifying transparency, as if I might be scoured away. So I ate. With or without Aida, whose hours in the lab stretched longer, I ate. I craved grease, density. My thighs rounded. My collarbones disappeared. A protective layer of fat swaddled me as gently as the macadamia milk I poured over charred spinach some days, braised duck on others, on messes of pine nuts and tarragon. The morning I found the bin of macadamias empty, I cried. Sought comfort in pistachios.

The cat responded, a little, to his new diet of raw meat. He shivered at the draft from the door, we two attuned to a calendar the residents ignored. They still came to dinner in wispy gowns and thin-soled shoes. My own silks no longer fit. New clothes arrived with a note: *You are at twenty-one or twenty-two. Reduce.* I hadn't seen my employer for weeks; he was on a tour of Kandinsky's plants. Very romantic.

One night I woke up slick, my whole body ringing, as if I had dreamed of Aida's breast in my mouth and not a panna cotta. I unfroze the last vat of cream. I stirred the caramel sauce I'd tasted in my dream, used the same mint sprig and square plate—but in my dream the plate had rested on a checked cloth in a cramped room, and the fans were rickety, the waiters jovial, the floor that particular sticky black of the dining room at La Ciccia.

Aida showed up and followed the recipe to the gram. She had the precision for pâtisserie I lacked. *Good?* she asked as I spooned into her panna cotta.

It's perfect.

I spoke the truth. But after she left I made two more batches, both unfaultable, both unsatisfactory.

Corn syrup, it struck me at four in the morning. The caramel sauce was made from corn syrup. La Ciccia was a red-sauce joint that served eight-dollar specials to college kids and off-duty construction workers. It had been a comfort to me to walk past and see the giant bottle of Karo glowing from the kitchen window, warm and liquid yellow.

———

I had no chance to share this revelation. Aida was on call in the lab, in constant consultation with her father, plans plans plans shaving her down to a narrow blade of efficiency. Our hours together shrank. As I would not serve bitter greens without the consolation of oil, so I began to keep back my less palatable feelings, awaiting a time when we would again sit languid over twelve courses, sharing as well the sweet, the fatty.

This sere, narrowing season. Aida stumbling into the restaurant to request foods she barely chewed, polentas and poached eggs, fruit butters straight from the jar. Or Aida, manic, hands fumbling a wine cork as she spoke in one unbroken sentence of breakthroughs and innovations, the benefits of Spanish mackerel over Atlantic, and the dynamics of the relocation committee comprised of herself, her father, Kandinsky, and two top investors. Over and over I heard of the need to balance human desire and ecosystemic health as the committee shaped a vision for its new home. Aida variously framed the debate as business versus science, efficiency versus exploitation, stability versus risk, laziness versus perseverance, idiocy versus intelligence. Never as father versus daughter. *We're close*, she said again and again, as if to convince herself. *I can see it, I can see it. Can't you?*

We lay side by side in the glass eye. But I didn't drink so much or rise so high. *I don't see it yet*, I told her.

As my employer declared more recipes optimized, not to be changed, I grew desperate to fill my time. On the basis of an offhand comment Aida made about curry, I spent weeks reconstructing a recipe by the world's best Indian chef, twenty-two spices compressed into a thumb-sized cookie that liquefied against the roof of the mouth. I candied summer's last fruits and presented them, tournéed to jewel-like facets, on a length of velvet. I was all night tinkering with a pad thai, wanting Aida to experience, as I had in an alley of old Bangkok, this precise magic of sugar and lime and fish sauce, knowing we wouldn't bring with us that variety of lime, that species of anchovy. But Aida failed to exclaim at the breath of the wok that smoked of equatorial nights. She said, *I've been up since five, you know.*

Fundamentally, ours was a disagreement about time. How much remained. What was most precious to preserve within its limits. One night, Aida showed up hours late to dinner. I can't remember what occasion I'd seized upon, an anniversary or minor holiday. She stole in like a thief. Past cold soup and congealed meat, past fork tines aglitter like milk teeth. *Forget dinner*, she said as she pushed her tongue past my recriminations. *I'm hungry for something else.* Her body, in from the night, was one cold angle, and her mouth stank of lies. I yanked her coat open. Out spilled the perfumed wrappers of another meal. I wept; I would have preferred an affair to a snack.

The sky ceased to be summer's clear pane. Storm clouds obscured and my staff awaited instructions as I stared out, unable to picture the next step in a recipe, or the pleasure in Aida's face. Beneath the whine of wind I heard the low-country howl of my old despair. When I think of the end of this year I don't see the braises and pot-au-feus on a laden table; I see the food dumped at the base of the mountain, putrefying.

I think there's something wrong with me, I confessed after another fight, another pot overturned between us, lentils pinging to the floor. She was not cruel; she did not want me to be right. *You'll feel better after a break*, she murmured into my hair. *Of course you're tired of the same thing day in and day out. Let the staff handle meals. I'll speak to my father.*

But I had taught them; they cooked only my employer's recipes. I asked if we could get off the mountain. Have lunch in Milan. *Please.*

My employer agreed, with stipulations. We would be discreet. We would not mention the mountain. We would take security detail with us, though Aida persuaded him to have our guards wait at the city border. Aida would not wear jewelry or furs and the dogs must accompany us at all times. We would don protective gear and submit to full-body decontaminations upon our return. *For your safety*, he said.

I pulled on jeans and a sweater for the first time in almost a year. A stranger faced me in the mirror. She wasn't some elegant idea of a woman, so thin as to dissolve into the spiritual. She stood on legs rounded and solid, firm to the earth.

Frump couture, Aida quipped when she picked me up. *Where in the world did my father find those clothes for you?*

They're my own. I see you took liberties with "discreet."

I'm wearing black! Long black duster, black boots, black gloves past the elbow, even her convertible was black. Yet the protective gear glittered as I unfolded my set. *Gold thread is naturally antibacterial.* Even Aida hadn't messed with the headgear, though. Our helmets weighed at least ten pounds. *To filter out microplastics in the smog.*

She'd brought a sack of apples, the last of a rare heirloom variety deemed unfit to take in our move. The lab had run the variables: too water-hungry, too small, the barest nugget of flesh trapped under a quarter inch of bitter, inedible peel. We dug out the honeyed pulp with our fingers. Aida flung peels at the security cars that trailed us. Did I know that there had once been eight thousand varieties of apple? Did I know apples were prominent in at least four mythologies? Did I know that in the Judeo-Christian one, an alternate translation of *apple* was *pomegranate*? Did I know that the island of Avalon, floating out of time and ruled by women, was said in one interpretation to be covered in apple trees? Did I know that Avalon—

Let's just drive, I said.

We didn't speak until we crossed the border and dipped, like seabirds, beneath the smogline. The gray shifted around us in awesome currents. We buckled our helmets on. As bare branches scraped the windshield, seeming to reach for the fruit in our laps, I felt obligated to mention that the food in Milan might be different from how I remembered it.

Of course, Aida exploded, breath misting her visor. *If it's panzerotti you're after, or risotto alla Milanese, we can bring someone up the mountain to teach you. This place*—she swept a hand to the shrouded horizon—*has nothing.*

It's a beautiful city.

We lived in Milano.

Do you miss it?

We left when nativists broke our windows and spray-painted MANGIA I RICCHI *on the door. That's "eat the rich."* We drove on. *I don't think of it at all.*

A hundred and eighty kilometers an hour, two hundred, and this time I leaned into the speed. Milan rose, hazy, from the smog. Leaving our security detail at the city limits, we whipped down narrow streets until stopped by a blockade. The center was closed to vehicles. Though Aida waved cash at a traffic cop, in the end we parked. She left the male dog inside the locked car. *To guard it.*

I'd expected a subdued city, dreary, like the British port town. Milan just turned up the lights. Billboards raised ten stories of incandescence, and piazzas rippled with pink and purple bulbs that lent a rakish, party mood. I wanted to linger at the shops, but Aida rushed ahead. She spoke loudly of doom and dimness as our stiff gear crackled with our steps. People stared. For the first time, I looked at her and felt shame.

Our helmets might be to blame, I pointed out. The visors muted colors and cut off peripheral vision. I couldn't get my bearings, taking wrong turn after wrong turn, Aida growing testier by the minute, until finally, I ripped my helmet off.

The city came in. It stank of smog and diesel and cooking oil; of dust, gone stale. A sudden waft of bleach made me cough. Aida shrieked as I took another breath, deeper. The rest of the laundry followed the bleach, wet fabric and soap, a milder, damp cloud. Musk and leather scudded in from a market doing brisk trade in those slaughtered cows. Somewhere: fresh tar, a new road. The female dog had her nose lifted, too; I turned, ignoring Aida's warning about pollutants, and traced the scent of jasmine to a knot of teenage girls. They gawped back. Their perfume was overapplied, like their makeup, cheap, synthetic stuff; but it was they who eyed my expensive gear with pity.

The city slapped me awake. This was no mountain breeze—that air so politely clean it functioned as a kind of anesthetic, too, numbing a person to garbage, ripely flowered; to new paint and old stone; and to a smell that unfurled like a pungent brown carpet, calling me down the road.

Come on, I said, breaking into a jog. Language changed as we entered Chinatown.

I'd visited once before, in my twenties, homesick and newly arrived to Europe. In that crabby, jetlagged state, I'd pushed through Italians who dawdled in the street, snapping their photos and gulping their dan dan mian with the carelessness of those for whom this was but one meal in an endless procession. I'd resented the facile culinary tourism; I'd resented the crowds. And then smog came down with its imperious hand. And then food, and Chinatown, were politicized by nativists, too.

This version of Chinatown was ghostly. Shopfronts sat boarded up, or shattered. Graffiti suggested that occupants had been hounded out. I stopped at one of the few stalls still open. Just a window in a dirty gray wall.

The menu, if you could call it that, was a series of scribbles and strikethroughs. Only one item remained. The vendor's hair was gray, too, as was the dubious batter in her mixing bowl. Yet the smell was a fist in my throat. I couldn't, quite, speak. I held up one finger.

What is it? Aida asked as the vendor ladled batter onto a smoking griddle. Behind its plexiglass partition, the stall displayed bags of mung bean flour, plastic tubs of powders and pastes. No sign of green. *Where does she source ingredients from? Who are her suppliers? Is her water clean?*

Jian bing, I had time to say, and then I was watching the vendor.

She bent over her griddle like a jockey or dancer, her body a spring. In swift sure strokes she painted the crisping batter with brown sauce, red sauce, a splash of egg substitute. Sausage flicked in pink slices from her palm, knife passing over bare skin, too fast to see. She didn't have to look to find her salt; she never moved her planted feet. She stood at her center and from there the steam expanded, fogging glass, blistering my cheeks, oversweeping the street and the smog and Aida with her doubts. The vendor raised a wrist to wipe her face. I saw the shine of a burn in the same spot as my own; I saw myself freed of protective gear, stripped to skin, fitted in a space wholly my own as the kitchen on the mountain never could be.

The vendor folded the bing. She offered us the warm, greasy package.

What——, Aida said, hanging back, so I took it.

I bite in.

We each have our moment in the olive grove, when the shabby dream of this world lifts and we slip into another. However straight the path may seem, however fixed the destination, there are ways and ways and ways. Cilantro curls my tongue in Milan and I sit at a table in Pasaje, facing a stack of gray jian bing. The color isn't mung flour, not yet, but buckwheat my mother got on sale, bitter and dry. This is long before the word *refire*, before I hear of Escoffier and his *Le Guide Cuisine*; in the quiet lonesomeness of night it is instinct that guides me. Through lunch meat and cold rice, Oreos snuck out of school in a napkin, past pickles flaccid beside jars of jelly and peanut butter. All my puny harvest. I don't know what I want until I taste it. Hours later I wake to the sound of my mother coming home from work. Her low voice. Her tired tread. Her face is dim, the kitchen too, but day breaks in our single window as she eats the breakfast I have made from what she made me, and her face: it dawns: a horizon I have never seen: I see: my mother knows pleasure. Hard-won, deep-buried, scraped from the dark of need, hers is a pleasure I find by seeking my own. I was raised to eat bitterness.

Aida, from the other place, is asking if I'm okay. I pass the bing, hear her helmet unlatch at last. She chews, and chews, coming to meet me, bite by bite.

We ordered seconds. Thirds. Nibbling, sniffing, considering, I guessed that the batter was mung-protein flour, that the sauce I'd smelled was brewed from fermented beans, that the sausage slipped in soy substitute for pork. I knew, beyond a doubt, that there was plenty of dried cilantro. *I'm missing something*, I was forced to admit. *Mung flour should leave the bing bitter.*

Aida was up at the window before I could stop her. The vendor listened, stoic. Disappeared. I explained how closely chefs guarded their proprietary recipes, how we'd insulted the woman. *You're wrong*, Aida said. *She'll come back with her price.*

We were both wrong. The vendor reemerged with a nondescript jar that, unscrewed, released a familiar odor

I said to her, *My mom liked peanut butter on her bing, too.*

Hazelnut butter, Aida corrected me once she'd performed the back-and-forth translation. She read from the label on the jar: thirty-two percent ground Italian hazelnuts, padded with almonds, mung starch, stabilizers, substitute sweeteners. *Emulsified*, Aida intoned, *hydrogenated, processed*, as I mimed, to the vendor, taking a very small bite.

The woman scooped a glob the size of a golf ball. The dog watched, mournful, as I accepted the spoon. Smoothness lodged in my throat, thick as memory. When I opened my eyes, the vendor was still holding out her jar.

She yelled after us as we walked away, heavier by several spoonfuls of nut butter, plus a fourth bing in Aida's pocket, one we hadn't been allowed to pay for. Aida translated: this was the last of the peanut butter. I thought we'd finally hear the woman's price. What she issued was an invitation, or maybe a challenge: come back in a week, when the new bing recipe would be better still.

Once more through city streets, this time Aida bare of face. *Don't tell my father.* So she is not her father's daughter, not employee or performer or object of desire. Not savior. What remains is just Aida. Her head turns, light on her shoulders, as we walk concrete and cracked tile. No mountain, no fields, no sun or stars, but oil shimmers in slick puddles, and a radio emits its crackling radiance: some generic pop song. The smog has thickened. I see, in pieces, her hair, teeth, throat. Rendered anonymous, she warms to it, whipping her head back, stomping like any girl on any dance floor. The shops turn up their artificial lights, and the gray blooms with pinks and purples so unlikely it seems we float through the atmosphere of some softer planet, far far behind us countries and borders, continents and politics, our despoiled inheritance of earth. She grabs my hand. We dance until the song is over.

What remains is her voice, panting, quick, as she says, *Why did you choose French food?*

I give the easy answers: that it was a requirement for this job, for every job I'd wanted, that French cooking, not Chinese, spelled success. Across the years it is hard to make out this version of myself so blinkered by ambition that she sprinted through thirty years without asking why. But Aida, exacting, infuriating, points out the forty-five thousand Chinese restaurants in pre-smog America, and for the first time I pause in the space between my past and my future.

I wanted to cook real food. She asks if I mean authentic, and I have to laugh at the antiquated word. It belongs to a world in which *authentic* was a buzzword like *organic* or *local*, in which diners tracked the boldest spiciest most exotic as they might have hunted big game on safari. Then staple crops withered under smog. Then those recipes proved too brittle to survive the changing of the world. *Forget authentic. Peanut butter jian bing is real food. So are the hot dogs I grew up microwaving over rice, and even the menu at those fancy Chinese restaurants that once existed in cities like New York, the ones that could charge eighty bucks for truffle fried rice.* Such restaurants were as mythical as sphinxes to a girl from Pasaje, California, a town just large enough for one Jade Garden and one Le Bistro du Chat. Guess which served what. No chance you'd mistake them. One a door to a grease-stinking room of claustrophobic dimensions, the other swinging wide to show not just collared shirts and unaccented English, not just linens and sixty-dollar chickens, but a wide bright world in which value was ascribed to food made not for sustenance, not out of obligation or need, but out of love: real food. One day, I'd believed, I would, having proven my worth, arrive at my own space in a city capacious enough for coq au vin and truffle fried rice too, those New Yorks and Londons and San Franciscos. But that species of restaurant went extinct in the smog. Here I am, a hungry ghost in Milan, stomach churning with bing yet not quite full; here I am with a new hunger spiking like vinegar through the old as I say, *Real food is whatever cooks are proud to make. My nightmare was that I'd end up in some Jade Garden plating up someone else's bland, bored, mushu chop-suey illusion of what food is supposed to be. I know restaurants have to serve certain dishes to survive, it's not always a choice—but it's an insult to cooks. To diners, too. I refused to be stuck.* In Pasaje, California. In the smallness of my mother's life. In a fixed notion of my cooking, my abilities, my worth as ascribed to my Chineseness my Asianness my smallness my womanness my perpetual foreignness—myself. *French cuisine is respected everywhere. To earn the chance to cook real food, I needed that respect.*

And now you have it.

She is so sure, I less so. I think of the table on the mountain. The applause. I think of who stands applauding over faultless dishes served on the white porcelain that is still called china. As I think of the béchamel I've made a hundred times, how many thousands more, the *Yes* congeals on my tongue. I at that table I in that kitchen I with abundance at my feet: I am arguably the world's best French chef. But I think of the fat that seals the rillettes my employer has just declared perfected, not to be changed, a recipe to preserve the same satisfied stupor in all the worlds to come, and I cannot say yes. *French food seemed like the only way.* For the first time, I admit, *I didn't, exactly, choose.*

A sound found us through the smog. The female dog was first to hear it, pricking her ears. Thin and faint, then rising, insistent, a distant canine voice spoke of danger. The spell of the day broke as Aida dropped my hand and sprinted, her dog beside her.

I caught up at the car, where I found them swarmed by dozens, maybe hundreds, of children. Impossible to keep count in the smog. My mind went to car thieves, muggings, violence—but as it turned out, the children wanted to see the dogs.

A cheer went up when Aida unlocked the car and the hounds, reunited, raised their sleek red heads to bay. The warning went ignored. Hands reached to stroke those bright pelts, those soft, irresistible ears. *We're boxed in*, Aida said in frustration, in growing panic, and as the dogs, snarling, backed up against the car, their color gave me an idea.

I lobbed our remaining apples as high and hard as I could. The children looked up. Saw: red. They scattered to give chase.

Let them have it, I said when Aida groused. *The poor little bastards. That's the last time they'll taste anything so good.*

I can't see for shit down here. She wiped the windshield, lowered the roof of the convertible for better visibility. Glancing around, she said as she pulled out, *I wouldn't issue invitations to your pity party just yet.*

Milan bloomed with a fragrance of lost orchards, honey and hives and wine, as children bit into fruit—and then, incredibly, spat. *Those are the palates you're so afraid to disrespect*, Aida shouted. It was hard to hear her above the sound of children giving voice to their distaste.

Their mouths seemed whole, their teeth and wits intact as they followed us down the street. Spitting, ducking, screaming at exaggerated decibels when hit, they flung our priceless apples. To add insult to injury, one boy who clutched his stomach in grotesque exaggeration was actually eating a sandwich. He straightened up, bowed. Took a dusty bite of bread. I watched with horror and incredulity and a righteous superiority that slowly gave way to something else. Each time his mouth distended around gray bread: sheer bliss. I craned. Couldn't see between the limp slices. Couldn't imagine what, baked or boiled or stewed or fried, might elicit such delight. Aida was right: I didn't pity the children. Suddenly I envied them their knowledge of something better than apples, than milk, than honey.

I stumbled out of the slow-moving car. The apples in the gutter were bruised, nasty. I found my target: a scrawny girl who watched from the sidelines with frank hunger. I took the last, perfect fruit from the pocket of my protective suit. Knelt down. Eyes on the girl's, I peeled back the bitter skin. Mimed eating the flesh.

I held the apple out. Was there ever a girl who could ignore that color?

I did try to tell you, Aida said, not without regret, as the girl fled, spitting pulp and obscenities. *Research has been done on this phenomenon.* As I got in the car, she referenced a turn-of-the-century study on children raised eating fast foods. Their tongues were left calloused, unable to distinguish between more subtle flavors. *The sample size was small, but directionally useful. These palates are ruined, too.* I half-listened. My eye was on the girl, still savaging the hated apple. She threw its pulp to her feet. Somehow she'd misunderstood. Somehow I must make her understand. If only she knew—

She broke off a piece of peel. Red, it was, and so thick, so bitter, it had consigned the fruit to extinction. She lay it on her tongue like a communion wafer. Her face—

The arrogance of her, Aida said as I lost sight of the girl in the crowd. *Our recipe will be exponentially better.* She was speaking of the vendor, and of jian bing. Our heirloom beans and einkorn wheat, our Valencia peanuts and macadamias. *Did you hear me? Macadamias. We're bringing them after all.* I put my fingers to my lips, trying to discern from them any trace of the apple peels we'd flung by the dozen to the roadside. *Okay, to hell with macadamias, I suppose. Never mind that I spent days arguing their case to the relocation committee. Is it marconas you prefer now? Say the word and I'll grow almonds, or cashews, whatever nuts you want. Not like I have anything better to do with my time. I'll invent new crossbreeds. If you'd just. Fucking. TELL ME.*

The car's horn shattered the air. It was the sound of the violence that had hovered all autumn around our fights, our careful lovemaking. It screamed; it wailed. The children fell quiet. *I'm not blind*, Aida said. *I know you're unhappy. Tell me what it'll take.*

It was late in the day, late in the year. Late. On certain mornings the air of the mountain acquired a silvered edge, so clear it could cut. I met Aida's eyes.

I had lied when I said I could not see her vision. How could I not see it, alive in the eyes of her. Green above a filthy world she'd plant pomegranates and date palms, macadamias and arabicas lush and dark with seed. Olives would shimmer gray to the horizon. A garden of glories, and within, a plot for me. She hadn't wavered. It was I who had changed.

I want more, I said, putting a hand to my stomach, which rides higher than most know. Closer to the heart. *I want the jian bing that vendor will make when she runs out of nut butter. I don't think she's arrogant. I think she's right. I want to sample jian bing from every cart in Beijing, and I want to taste what those kids are eating at home, what they don't teach in cookbooks at Le Cordon Bleu. There's so much out there—* Helplessly, I said, *I haven't even told you how much I love foods wrapped in other foods.*

Then tell me.

I tried. I tried. Banh xeo in Hanoi, I said, and duck folded in the translucent bing of northern China. I spoke of tacos in Mexico City: suadero, al pastor, gringas. South Indian dosas as long as my arm, thinner than the rib of a feather. *Oh, Aida,* I said when I fumbled the names of the chutneys. *How can I know all I'll ever want? Something will get left out. I was wrong about cilantro.*

Tlayudas, she said stubbornly, as if she hadn't heard. *Blini. Crêpes.*

They're basically French jian bing, I said with a strangled laugh.

Pita sandwiches.

Pickle roll-ups.

Calzone.

Bossam! I yelled, and the dogs barked and the children cheered and the streets of old Milan rang with the imported memory of pork kissed by brine, earthy with Korean bean paste, safe in its bed of red leaf lettuce.

So we'll come back to Milan for bossam, she agreed. *There were a few Korean restaurants before, though the diaspora wasn't large. Frankly, locating proper bossam will be a pain in the ass. Typical of you.* But she grinned as she spoke. *What the hell. I like a challenge. We have two years, right? I've been curious about red leaf lettuce.* She was seeing the type of problem she liked best, one that required calculations and clever stratagems, one that would expand the size of her garden plot.

But it would never be more than a garden, fenced and bounded.

And what happens after two years? I said. *It'll be me again, alone in a kitchen wherever we've gone. You were right the first day. I'm a mediocre cook. I'm not enough for this job. Not alone.*

You're enough for me. Softly we drifted through the darkening street. Night worked on Milan though the sun was not visible; we felt rather than saw the flux, the dimming that artificial light could not stave off. *I need you. As the project needs me. Together with my father, don't you see, we were made for this work. No one else can do what we do.*

Can you be human for one fucking second? The dogs rose on their haunches in warning. I lowered my voice. *What do you need, Aida? Not your father, not the committee. I don't give a shit about the project. Only you. You can't tell me you don't want to eat jian bing in Beijing. Bossam, just imagine it, in Seoul.*

I saw her lips part. Saw the gleam of saliva on her teeth. But she swallowed, and predicted the end of street vendors in another year. *Pessimist,* I named her, and she said, with scorn, *On what basis do you claim that this state of affairs will improve? Do you have studies our researchers aren't privy to? Share them if so. I'd like to see them. Really, I would. I would I would I would.* She bore down on the gas pedal, made the engine whine. *According to the trajectory of the data my father has procured, I am a realist. An optimist, if you ask the committee. They push back on my suggestions. They look at me and see a dumb, sentimental girl. But I can save more than they think possible. More than you think possible.* She clenched the wheel. *I will make it enough. I have to.*

I had no intelligence to offer her cool and brilliant brain, I who did not know what I thought until I tasted it. I had only this new-old hunger, this ache in the gut, this faith, inarticulate, in a next bite, and a next, and a next: bitter with flour or chewy with peel and pith, thick as love and alive with good decay. What hid in cupboards, what rotted belowground, what poison was made salvation by human ingenuity or desperation or arrogance of a form my mother might have approved. Wordless, I expressed myself in the only way I knew. I unwrapped our last jian bing.

It was cold by then, and dry. I warmed the bite in my mouth. Tongue to tongue I fed her. What, I ask, is fairness in a world that fears there is never enough, in which one need always scrapes against another? I'm not smart enough to give that answer. I only believe that the tongue, dumb beast, is not selfish in its instinctive cant toward pleasure. The question that follows me through the seasons of my life is what comes after hunger is sated; whether that pleasure is guarded, or shared. Aida chewed. I saw her eyes half-close, saw the wet on her lashes. Saw us driving down infinite roads to gather in our palms all the flavors of our lives, as scientists once gathered seeds. Worlds upon possible worlds bloomed from the pleasure that reflected between us, doubled, multiplied. As long as I live I will see my joy on her face, see her face as mine.

Neither of us saw the child reach in and grab a dog.

———

There is a rent in this day:
    Canine scream
    Aida's face turning from mine
    Wheel turning with her
    Car turning
    Blur of sky
    A thud.
    We come to a halt in the thick, set night.

Children scattered as the last apples rolled, smashed, beneath the tires. The air: overripe. Aida followed her dogs into the road. Full grown, they stood as high as my shoulder and the earth was dry beneath their paws except where it pooled, red. A child lay facedown. The dogs put snouts to damp mass. Aida's face became opaque to me, an alien material that the light fell strangely upon. *Control them,* I said. *CONTROL YOUR DOGS.* And then I remembered what could reach that place beyond language.

I slapped her. Her eyes went black. I saw the moment she ceased to see me. Two red forms left the child and stalked my way.

She whistled. They went to her.

My employer arrived with the security detail. Aida ran into his arms like a child. He spoke to the police, who in turn spoke to the medics, and the gathered crowd, and the mother who stood hurling apples and obscenities from behind yellow tape, who was not permitted forward until my employer nodded at the police who spoke to the medics who allowed the mother to clutch that small, limp hand. Aida roused only when an officer pointed to the dogs. She grasped her father's sleeve. A look passed between them, not tender as the gesture was, but assessing.

There was a moment when I thought she meant to speak to me; when, in the brief space between uniformed men, I saw her mouth lapse open. I couldn't bear to meet her eyes so like those of the man who stood behind her, his hand on her shoulder. I turned away, sickened. *My father and I, my father and I.*

My employer drove us back as Aida slept under sedation in the backseat. He explained that the incident had been ruled an accident. The boy had stabilized and would be discharged from the hospital by day's end, though he would be left disabled by the bleeding in his brain. That bleeding was a result of collision with the car, which witnesses agreed the boy had run into the road to follow. Neither driver nor dogs were responsible for that injury. I studied my feet, between which a binder spilled numbers and charts. My employer named the compensation he would pay the boy's family. He named the average household income of the region. He named the cost of raising each of the boy's three siblings, the cost of healthcare for aging grandparents, the cost of food and rent. *It is the best thing for them*, he said.

I asked if the best thing wasn't to take them where we were going. *Blood money*, I said again.

My money is more useful than your guilt, though you are welcome to offer it. The officials were curious about the involvement of a foreign national. Well?

I wish I could say I waited longer before I shook my head.

Correct. There is no justice in the mob. Italy for Italians, they say now. They did not consider my people Italian thirty years ago when the sea rose over the island. They turned us away from the shelters, never mind how many generations we'd lived and worked the land. They turned us away at gunpoint. As if we were criminals. I will not see my daughter imprisoned.

Then let her go. Aida slept, her face smooth; I couldn't remember the last time I'd seen her conscious and at peace. *You ask too much. She won't complain because she wants your approval more than anything, but you're breaking her. Let her slow down, at least.*

That was when my employer told me the truth, or part of it. I don't know why, given that my knowing presented no strategic value. I can only conclude that he, for his seeming calm, was shaken. *There is no time left.*

Allies had informed him that parliament meant to pass a piece of legislation that spelled the death of the mountain as we knew it. Acceding to the desires of its populace, Italy planned to take the strictest measures and reclaim the mountain, along with its intellectual property, in a year. All current residents, scientists, and staff were to be put out. It was the zoologist, that balked and furious man, who'd leaked documents so damning that even our allies could not justify voting any other way. *The man broke his nondisclosure agreement. I will bury him with lawyers, but that will not stop the proceedings. We are lucky Kandinsky spoke on our behalf. He bought some time. But in a year, they will chivvy us out like so much prey. Aida must ready our new home.*

Even in sleep, she shifted at her father's command. The blanket slipped from her shoulder. I reached to fix it. Stopped. The dogs had begun growling.

Fear can be useful, my employer said as he pulled over. The dogs let him adjust her blanket, smooth her hair. *Fear was the whetstone that sharpened the instincts of those who first dared to hunt mammoth, or sail across seas. There are times I fear the scope of my daughter's vision—but it is better to hold the gun.*

Is that all she is to you? I said, choking on it.

You know nothing. She is my *daughter.* That voice, its promised violence, rumbled through the car. *That family has three other children. She and I are all we have left. I know what she is meant for.*

He raised his hand. It trembled. A faint discoloration yellowed his first and second fingers. He trembled, and I should have seen it from the outset: the symptoms of an unreformed smoker. I offered him my pack. He twitched, then opened my door.

Besides the risk of cancer, he said as I slipped out, *it kills the tastebuds. Smoking is no fit habit for a chef.*

On the field in the shadow of the mountain I struck a match and thought back to before my first brunoise, my first mise en place, when I first learned to love this sip of death. I'd come to the kitchen with no skills and no reason to exist beyond a burning interior ambition. Smokers exist in every kitchen. It kills a tastebud or two but we all die, and no one knows better than those who club the fish, clean the guts from the meat, and serve for your delectation a plate from which all blood has been wiped. We cook despite bad pay and sore backs and inadequate sleeps in apartments we can't afford and we wake up choosing again that most temporary of glories that is made, and then consumed: we know. We all die. Whether it comes after thirty years of hard labor or sixty at a desk, whether we calculate or plan, in the end we have only the choice of what touches the lips before we go: lobster if you like it or cold pizza if you don't, a sip of smoke, a drink, a job, a reckless passion, raw fish, the beguilement of mushrooms, cheese luscious beneath its crown of mold. What sustains in the end are doomed romances, and nicotine, and crappy peanut butter, damn the additives and cholesterol because life is finite and not all nourishment can be measured. When I learned to smoke behind a restaurant, my breath curling toward an inconsolable sky, I learned what it means to live by the tongue, dumb beast, obedient to neither time nor money, past nor future, loyal to a now worth living. I took my cigarette to the filter, and for the first time I appraised my employer back. He claimed to have evolved past fear. He lied. Behind the mask was a damp, scared boy. Fear of toxins, fear of carcinogens, fear of flood and smog and protest and entropy and all that could not be optimized, controlled, bought and held behind glass. Fear fueled a country so intent on perfection that they would give up the world.

Aida came down with food poisoning. For residents, I acted out motherly concern. To my employer, I delivered bland apologies. In truth, I wanted her guts to twist, her stomach to revolt. I wanted illness to smash through hard smooth surety and set her free.

She sent a note.

I'm craving steamed eggs. Something easy on the stomach. Do you know the Korean version? Her handwriting was girlish, looped. *Please.*

There was no secret message. I crumpled the page. No further notes came, nor Aida herself.

It was winter when I laced my running shoes and left the restaurant under the guise of health. I had last run with the dogs, toward the protection of a country whose purpose I failed to understand; I'd been lighter then, swept along.

I left the door open. The cat only tucked into himself, saving strength. He knew what he sought was not to be found on the mountain. We were more alike than I'd admitted. *Almost there*, I said, stroking a knuckle down the fine bone of his skull.

I meant to run down every road and up to every house if necessary. Movement conjured appetite, specific and sharp. For carne asada fries sweating in Styrofoam. For Australian fairy bread doused in sprinkles so plastic they'd outlast the coral reefs. For jian bing and soy milk and man tou strung each morning down Beijing's hutongs, where vendors were rumored to whiten their dough with lead paint, not fatal in such quantities, but sweet, addictive, you could cultivate a dangerous passion. *Every artist needs a muse*, the pastry chef had said, and it occurred to me that the muse might be myself.

I ran ten miles, twenty, a hundred. My thighs banded with muscle and girth. At last I found the meteorologist's house.

He was packing when I let myself in. He didn't stop when I spoke my real name. *I knew something was fishy*, he said between the tape in his teeth. *So you're an actor. What does it matter now?*

A chef, I said, and told him I was number three on the list. He was a hundred and eleven. One hundred and ten residents would make the move, along with another hundred support staff. The meteorologist shoved a box aside and faced me. He looked ten years older in his hostility, his features lined with unhappy suspicion. Again he asked why he should care. *I'm giving up my spot*, I said.

He was a long time responding. *What do you want in return?*

I'm contractually obligated to keep my secret. If you expose me, I'll be fired through no fault of my own. You get the spot. I get severance.

So it's about money. His suspicion eased. *Still*— Rumor had it that my employer had secured a site beneath the Arctic permafrost capable of outlasting a nuclear scenario. Surely no amount of cash could compete with that. The meteorologist badgered me for rationale. Logic.

I shrugged. *I'm craving a decent California burrito.*

He thought this over, then shook his head. He tore off a flap of cardboard. A seven, he wrote, a zero, and then his hand went back, hiding the numbers as he erased, rewrote, reconsidered. He took his time. His jaw, when he handed this folded note to me, was set. Uncompromising. I had to tug the cardboard from his grip.

It wasn't a dollar amount, or a bribe. He'd written directions. An address.

My uncle's spot in Little Persia. He marinates his carne asada in advieh. The meteorologist's expression grew more pugnacious still. *And no, I don't want to hear about La Palma, or Tito's, or that line about going to San Francisco for a real burrito. His are the best in the state. Double-check those directions—it's either exit seven, or seventeen. It's worth the effort. I practically lived on those things until the age of eighteen.*

Dumbfounded, I said the first thing that came to mind. *I thought you were from Ira—*

He raised an eyebrow. I flushed. Et tu, Brute?

Tucking the address away, I asked if he didn't want to eat his uncle's burrito for himself. True to form, my employer had confirmed that there would be no leaving the new, self-sufficient home.

The meteorologist looked out the window. West. *I won't waste my life waiting for the US to open its borders.* Anti-Muslim sentiment was high; however low my spot on America's waitlist, the meteorologist sat lower. Though he'd shipped date seeds back to family in Los Angeles, he could not put his body on a plane. *If I have a chance to study anticyclones under the northern lights, and see what no one else in my field has seen—*

I think of his face tipped back to cloudy sky. There were others on that mountain, too.

The meteorologist, as he walked me to the door, delivered a warning about safety. I assured him I'd be fine. He pointed outside and asked if I knew the story of the sedge.

The grass had been planted, the meteorologist said, the spring after Eun-Young's first attempt to leave her husband. She had renovated a family estate in the Korean countryside, meaning to take Aida, just thirteen, with her. But the building burned down under mysterious circumstances despite the wetness of the winter. After Eun-Young returned, my employer covered the mountain in imported Korean grasses. Every blade was the mark of a guilty man.

True or not, I said, *he let her go in the end.*

The meteorologist looked at me with something like awe. *You really don't know a thing, do you? We believed he'd slit Eun-Young's throat.* He touched his own. *When Aida disappeared, we figured she'd done something to displease him—that he'd had her killed, too. People expressed serious doubts. Most were ready to pack up, groundbreaking research or no. I don't think there'd be a single investor if you hadn't proved Eun-Young was alive.* He paused. *I hope you were paid what you're worth.*

I'd been so proud of negotiating a few thousand more for my bonus, so sure of my intelligence, my command. I'd forgotten that a scam relies on the desire of the scammed to believe what she wants to believe. The game had always been my employer's to win.

Eleven

❧

I was not killed, I was not hunted. My time in that country died a natural death as the year went out. The meteorologist seeded his rumors with care. Gossip, damp ruminations, suggestions of rot until, like a storm cloud too heavy to stay aloft, my identity split open. My employer did not respond to allegations. He simply called Sunday dinners to a halt. If I had hoped in some part of me for upheaval, for a different release of Aida's obligations, I did not get that satisfaction. By this point all remaining residents had been converted into investors, their money well and inescapably enmeshed in the country. Their names were on the list: they no longer required the pretense of Eun-Young.

I had little to distract me from the cat's worsening condition. Though his stomach continued to protrude, his fur fell out in patches. I moved him like a houseplant into sunnier spots, regretting that I had not taken Aida's offer to have him seen.

Mail came addressed to my name. I was a cunt, several species of insect, a prostitute—either very cheap or very expensive, depending on who wrote. Residents who'd exhibited no prior fluency took care to express disgust in English.

A few notes were kind. A Spanish tycoon who'd failed to make the list offered the position of private chef on his estate in Chihuahua, Mexico, and I spent a blissful evening entertaining fantasies of a drive to the American border. The meteorologist sent more LA restaurant recommendations as they occurred to him: mapo tofu lasagna, cheese wheel pasta just for the spectacle of it, pupusas, cha gio, tahdig from his uncle's sit-down establishment, neither of us dwelling on whether these restaurants still existed. The kitchen staff were given orders to ignore me. But sometimes, in passing, they could not avoid looking at me, at *me*. Once, I was even offered a smoke.

My last meeting with my employer was brief. He summoned me to a dining room repurposed to hold his computers and charts. On the shelves I glimpsed Plato's *Republic*, genetics textbooks, tomes embossed with *Utopia*. Chrome cities gleamed on covers.

I should fire you for breach of contract. He didn't look up from what he was writing. My contract lay open not to the nondisclosure agreement but to a minor clause I'd skimmed. Among various standard job requirements were criteria for hygiene, grooming, and weight. *Yet my daughter insisted that we give you severance.*

His pen pushed into paper. How deep the grooves, how quiet the anger worn into this man who would forever measure himself against the expectations of those who found him lacking. I was wearing my old sweater, a pair of faded pants. I'd gained twenty pounds since entering the country and felt stronger than I had in years, clearheaded. My employer offered a new contract. A lesser role, no face time at meals, but a spot on the list. I refused. At last he gave me his full attention.

The same cold, eternal black eye. The face around it wore its exhaustion. *You would not do this if you understood what Eun-Young's departure did to her.*

And what did you do to Eun-Young?

He held the door for me, another of his rituals. He liked to stand too close, positioning himself between door and guest, so that a person must bend and scurry under his arm, or else be forced to make a request of him. I declined to do either. As I squeezed past my employer, head held high enough to brush his sleeve, he reminded me that opportunities were rare for people like me. *People like us,* he may have said. He left a narrow gap, as if I were much thinner, as if I were still Eun-Young, and then, when I was between him and the heavy door, he took a step forward. There was no malice on his face, no triumph, only the cool impersonal gaze of a creature for whom such acts are instinct. His chest crushed mine. His shoulder smothered my face. As the breath was pressed out of me I caught his cologne: citrus and sedge, the scent of his stationery. No hand went to my neck, no nails dug the soft of my cheek. There was no sound, no speed, no blow, and all these years later I still find it hard to name this as violence, I still see the continued logic of the role for which I'd been paid: a person reduced and reduced and reduced till this bloodless erasure was the natural end. I gasped, feeling my lungs struggle, and fail, to expand. He pressed, inexorable. My vision darkened, dancing motes. I said, *Aida.*

The pressure eased. I became aware of the rug under my knuckles, the wheeze of my breath as I lay against the door. At his desk, my employer had resumed writing. He did not look as I, bent around my aching chest, walked out.

You know, I said when I was across the threshold. *I don't think you're an apex predator at all. You're a parasite.*

He told me to shut the door.

Later, I checked the dates. I met with my employer around the time that Kandinsky withdrew from the venture and funds began to grow tight. Predator had become scavenger, become vestigial. Perhaps it was the same day I saw him, and the hand that bore down with such force was penning a response to Kandinsky. That's probably fanciful thinking. Time and again I have tried to imagine my employer reading the missive that told him of Kandinsky's deposits halted, Kandinsky's factories ceasing production of parts; I have tried to imagine how he shared this news with his daughter. Calmly or furiously? As a parent comforting a child? As an employer chastising an employee? Did he tell her at all, or, as I have come to think over the years, was it his hand that balled up the note, his hand that hid the facts, his hand alone that swept the first bit of dirt over the grave? Hard as I try to follow the steps of that efficient, ruthless mind, I cannot. My foot slips. He is far ahead with the rest of them, so far I cannot see it.

Aida—

I see her all too well.

I put off saying goodbye. On my last day in the country, it was she who drove up in a car of uncharacteristic discretion. Gray. Quiet. Soft-shoed she stopped on the threshold.

You shouldn't be doing that, she said.

Yeah, yeah, lung cancer, tastebuds. I blew the smoke away from her. *Don't worry, I'm almost done.*

Take your time. She leaned against the door. *I don't mind the smell. It reminds me of . . .*

Charcoal? Coffee?

I'm not an idiot. I knew this whole time. She reached over. *It smells like you.*

She was prim, nervous, and very young as she took her first ciga-rette. She accepted a match as she'd accepted other morsels from my hand. One last time I watched her face light up: skepticism and trepida-tion and surprise and distaste and focus and then pleasure, as soft and new as an animal stepping aboveground. I watched her smoke. It was December. There was a different quality to the light, colder, more pierc-ing. I thought it might actually snow. She held her eyes wide as she in-haled and I saw that they were not, quite, perfectly black. They warmed in the ember's glow. *Don't tell my father,* she said as she coughed, ex-haled, adjusted, relaxed, showing me yet another face: a smoker's, transgressive and private, thrilled at her own defiance, let loose to be no longer perfect.

Are you that scared of him? I asked.

It's been different around here. After the incident with the chief zoolo-gist, Aida had been removed from the relocation committee, her scope of work reduced, her top-level security clearances denied. *But scared? Don't be ridiculous. He's not a complete monster.*

I unbuttoned my sweater. Bruises spattered, mottled fruit, across my chest. She stared, and I knew she knew when she looked away. *God, is he a fucking idiot,* she said in pale imitation of her old spirit. *But, you know, you have to choose your battles. He has a temper, yeah. So do I.*

You're not him. I left my sweater open despite the cold. *Aida, listen to me. You're not him. You don't have to go along with this.*

She picked at ragged cuticles. *However many his flaws—and trust me, I see plenty—at the end of the day, he protected me in Milan. He pro-tected both of us. You have to see the bigger picture. He and I—* She shook her head as if to loose the words. *He's seen me at my worst and never judged me. Never. My father, I—what do I have if he abandons me too?*

There is a part of me that lives in the waiting hush around this question. A part of me that I wish wiser, kinder, less myopic. Now I see the gnawed skin of her fingers and the fear behind her eyes, the question behind the one she asked. I might have spoken the words that released her from the mountain's spell. I did not.

You and your father, I said, bitterly.

I waited for you. You never came.

Neither did you.

She closed her lips around her cigarette like an expert. Inhaled. The look on her face—

We went in. I was packed, except for the cat. She asked where I was headed. Maybe Mexico, I said as I searched under furniture. Paris, if they'd let me in. I'd heard that parts of Switzerland were balmy, fringed by occasional light. *I probably have relatives in Beijing and Seoul. Maybe I'll go someday. Meet me there?*

Would if I could.

For her I guessed the tip of Chile, or Finland, or a facility dug into Arctic permafrost. She looked out at the wintry field, she didn't answer. What was it, Aida, that hung on the jags of your silence? Did you know? Did you know? Did you know?

Want to know what I have for you? She reached into her coat. *Our first ramps.*

My eyes prickled at the rank green odor. She was easy to mishear if you listened to words alone, to the clang of armor forged by need. But she had, too, this other language dispensed through food, encoded in observations of what fed me. I might have misunderstood had I not grown up versed in that vocabulary: my mother buying full-price Pop-Tarts for my first day of school, my mother leaving a bowl of cut fruit out after a fight. The lamplight off those facets. The radiance.

The smell of the ramps brought the cat out of hiding. I dove for him as Aida, with a hint of her old pride, described how she'd persuaded the committee to make space for this vegetable. *I may be on the outs, but I will never quit championing biodiversity.* We spoke of onions, leeks, the best way to store alliums. But when I asked what would happen with the seeds not chosen, when I suggested she pass the remainders to me, she erupted. *What can you do with your degree in fuzzy feelings?*

We were quiet. She ran a hand through her hair. She said she'd try, and that gave me courage for my real request.

I held the cat out. He was belly and bones. *Will you take him for me? You'll do a better job than I have. And if you're right about what happens to the world—I'd rather he be with you.*

Her face wrenched. *He won't last long enough to worry about that. Get him checked. Most vets will say one or two years.*

I thought back to the lab tech who'd delivered my lost cat, who'd refused to look me in the eye. Down the long corridor of gray years another small light went out. Why hadn't she told me, I asked, and she hesitated, she held herself back; and then, for the last time, she took my face in her hands. The last touch was different. No lust heated the breath that fell on my cheek; there was no friction, no desire in the thumb that ran over my lips, wiping my tears. She responded to my cry of pain as sexlessly, as assiduously, as helplessly as she did to a hurting sparrow or hound, and I had my answer to what the chimp had felt when she cupped its golden cheek. Whatever her stance on species and ecosystems, however severe the standards to which she held herself, held us all: this was the experience of an individual lucky enough to fall into her hands. This care. Rage I might against her contradictions, against hypocrisy's dulling bite; but this was, if not an answer, a truth.

I wanted you to be happy, she said when my face was dry of tears. *That's all I ever wanted. You probably hate me for it now.*

I don't hate you, Aida.

She wiped her hands on her sweater. Tucked them into her pockets, her armpits, at a loss. There was the cat, lounging, insouciant, the only one who didn't know the news of his condition. She knelt. Laid hands over two bald patches, as if to warm them. I joined her. Between us, the cat looked, briefly, whole. *I really am sorry,* she said as the cat began to purr. *It's a bad habit. My mother believed that ignorance is bliss. She liked to say we would have been spared all the ugliness of the world if Eve hadn't eaten that apple. I told her I'd always eat the apple.*

I would, too. And the pomegranates, and the jian bing, and Doritos, and all the rest. I cleared my throat. *Thanks, by the way. For the severance. I have choices now.*

See? People. Give them a choice and they'll always pick wrong.

She didn't always know best, I said, sharply, and to my surprise she conceded the point. Coaxing the cat into her lap, she told me about her failed visit to the family of the injured child. She'd taken bread baked with her own hands, a congratulatory gift for the boy's miraculous escape from injury. Superficial head wounds bled heaviest, her father had said, and the child had made a full recovery. The bread was fresh, plumped with the mountain's grain. There was an apology on her tongue. But before she could reach the house, a mob on the road slapped her loaf to the dirt. They shouted at her to get out. *You see, they want us to leave. This is the right decision.*

I didn't correct her, or tell her to demand the truth from her father.

What Aida would have done with that information is the question that burns and burns in the ruins of that field of my life. You see, I wanted her happy, too. *I bet it was good bread*, I said.

I could make more. It's an eighteen-hour proof. We can have it for break-fast tomorrow.

I can't.

It's my birthday next week. January. Stay just till then?

Her face was furious when I reminded her I was leaving. But it was in the smallest of voices that she said, *Maybe some other year, then. When we're old and lax and I've done everything I need to do, maybe, one day, you can come see what I've made. Try my bread. Bring me your jian bing recipe. Beijing and Seoul sound nice. Maybe—*

I never spoke to her again.

I saw her everywhere a year later. By then I was in Paris. The severance had appeared in my bank account, an amount larger than any I'd seen, far larger than stipulated in my contract, as terrifying as the sky had felt upon my arrival in the land of milk and honey. With that money came a French permanent residency card and a note. *Sorry it's not America, but at least you have freedom fries.* For a long time I rehearsed my retorts should I manage to slip again past the closed gates of that mountain. I wondered if I'd miscalculated, undervaluing her generosity and overindexing on my own vainglory. I rented a hotel room and imbibed as many vices as I desired. I didn't buy a phone or computer, didn't reach out to old contacts, the world too tremblingly large.

I left only at night. The cat declined to come. I wandered into neighborhood bistros with menus shorn short; and cafés with their umbrellas folded up, skeletal; and the occasional restaurant gastronomique such as Paris still maintained for purposes of national pride. Dusty velvet. Good china. Servers with the ravaged faces of war vets. From time to time, when drunk or desperate enough to put aside my dignity, I knocked on the door of the kindest-looking house on the street and asked for a bite of their dinner. My cash thrust into the warmth, my heart leaping in my throat.

I was out one night—poorly lit brasserie, single patron at the bar—when I saw her on the television.

Monte-le, I said, choking on a crouton. The bartender reached for the volume with such agonizing slowness that I thought I might actually die of waiting, of the stale bread in my throat, of the sight of Aida. Her face was flattened by the screen, the image cropped so that no trace of flamboyant outfit showed. My employer's face followed, the meteorologist's face, the faces of diners I'd served. Last and most lingering was the face of the sky in that country, a face I knew with a pang behind my eyes. Blue-white, heartrending, cloudless. I couldn't hear the television. I heard only Aida's voice, full of echoes as if from within a glass eye, saying, *Never again on all the earth.* The rocket rose from a dock that opened beneath the empty field at the base of the mountain. It rose in its clarity up toward a new world, it moved in terrible surety, and then, when it had all but disappeared, it bloomed. A year after I left the country the skies gave birth to a cloud that wasn't plumped with life-giving rain but fire and brimstone and, it seemed to me, the baying of red, red dogs as the ship exploded onscreen.

I ran out. I looked up. The bartender followed, hanging on my arm. I turned on him, snarling, I could have torn his throat out with my teeth. But his needs were so solvable. I pushed money into his hands.

Later I would understand that what I saw in the bar was a replay, that I'd had no chance of catching her in my sky. Later I would buy a

laptop and read theories about the explosion. That the engine had been
hastily completed in a second-rate factory after Kandinsky dropped out.
That the Mars colonization project had neglected to adhere to standard
test launches, relying on simulations and projections from earlier ves-
sels thanks to lack of funding. That it had launched a year ahead of
schedule for fear of losing its site at the mountain's base. That passengers had not been told of the neglected protocols. Deeper theories,
wilder. That passengers had been drugged and loaded aboard uncon-
scious. That passengers had known and were part of a freaky death cult
or human breeding venture. That the Italian government had sabotaged the project. That the laborers who'd built the vessel and been
denied spots aboard had sabotaged it. That there had been too many
passengers, too many animals, too many plants, too much weight of
life, too much greed, too much optimism, too much cynicism to ever
reach Mars. That some passengers survived the explosion. That passengers never boarded at all. That the owner of the vessel, a busi-
nessman with a long criminal record of scams, had proceeded with
the doomed launch because he had no other way to escape his debts,
and that he himself, along with his daughter, never boarded the ship.
That they lived on under new identities. Aida's picture was central to
many theories. Innocence and tragedy were applied to her young face
like makeup, falsening it, cheapening its substance. I imagined her high
in that void, driving at last toward a ferocious momentum that stripped
her of what kept her earthbound, a weightlessness she could not find in
dance. She would slip at last into the extravagant beauty of a world
infinite in choices, a world she had willed into being with savage intelligence and need. We all die. We have only the choice, if we are privileged, of whether death comes with a whimper or a bang; of what
worlds we taste before we go. I thought she chose the bang. More rarely

did I allow myself to remember her love of torrone and terrine, her face screwed up in the ugly joy of dance, and thought—

I saw her face everywhere, Aida but not like her, plastered up again and again till it became smooth and strange, a cipher without any meaning.

Twelve

❧

I lived for five more years in Paris. The explosion unfroze me. Eventually I shut my laptop and bought, in the hilly eighteenth arrondissement, an apartment from which I could stare out to the horizon. I'd witnessed green recently enough to believe.

The Mars colonization project remade the world, if not quite in the way she had envisioned. Its catastrophic failure achieved what morality had not: it gave pause to the wealthy. Dozens of space escapes that had brewed in secret took a step back. No one wanted to die by rushing ahead, and no investor wanted to lose all capital in doing so. A famous hedge fund manager went on TV to lambast the impracticality of putting all one's hopes and savings into a single, high-risk venture. He said, *There is wisdom in a diversified, time-tested solution.* By solution he meant earth, by time-tested he meant earth, but the language of business moved businessmen. Private funding poured into research on air purification and crop development; and while it is true that 80 billion euros went into the technology that cleared the smog, while it is true that the solution would not otherwise have been so quickly distributed, it is not true, as investors came to say, that they saved the world. It is not true to say that of any human. The Iranian American meteorologist's old lab at Berkeley was only the conduit for an innovation belonging to a species of dandelion. The weed had found a way to bind simple sugars to particles of smog, thus nullifying them. By the time this mutation was discovered, it had been occurring naturally, quietly, for years. Cloud-seeding technology left dark grains drifting down like spores over cities.

I was alive to see the story change, from one of humility and dazed gratitude to one of pride at the triumph of human good—a pride made possible by its contrast to human evil. Cheers rang through the streets the day my employer was named guilty of two hundred and nine counts of murder; deliberation took eight minutes. From my fifth-floor apartment, the sound of a happy mob was indiscernible from an angry one, and I bolted my door, swallowed a pill, slept under the heavy old fear of being cast out. The verdict was clear. I walled off my past. By the time reporters came knocking, I'd built a tomb sturdy enough to contain that mountain. My public apology renounced, in one swift paragraph, him, them, the mountain and my role on it. Anonymously, I donated the extra seeds I'd brought out of that country, along with a hard drive labeled FINDINGS in girlish script. I tried to move on.

Former residents proved a wrinkle in my plan. As they circulated through the media with highly varied accounts of events and villains that grew to match the public's appetite, I saw a version of myself become a surprising point of alignment. Someone was needed for the role of sympathetic victim, and residents expounded on my frailty, helplessness, childish naïveté as to the goings-on. My food, they generously agreed, was fantastic.

I opened a midpriced restaurant in Paris that served the kind of cuisine that would become commonplace, Italianish and Chinese Americanish for a new age. Chili oil and ricotta shared space with mung flour, dandelion greens, ash. As the first of its kind, my restaurant was a minor success. It expanded to half a dozen locations before young and hungry chefs came flooding back into Paris.

They outcooked me. Years of privation had molded their palates into odd, exquisite formations. They employed beurre blanc as easily as earthworms and canned beans. They'd foraged fungi from junk heaps and toasted protein powder for crunch. I ate at one such establishment when it was just a pop-up. Bare walls, mismatched silver. But when I bit into my entrée new universes flared one after the other like flags drawn from a magician's hat, a perturbation of worlds inhabited during famine as I, on a mountain, reproduced the food of past empires. Bitterly, and then gladly, I acceded to the new generation. Ironically, my role as restaurant investor won more acclaim than my actual cooking. Young chefs praised my solidarity, kindness, radicalism, foresight, et cetera— but the root was no more and no less than my private hunger. Here were the tastes I couldn't have imagined on my own. It was for this that I had traded a kingdom.

Years later, the United States reopened its borders with an apology for the agricultural tests that had contributed to smog. With its workforce depleted by famine, the country once again sought to make itself a home for immigrants. Wealthy, desirable, and debt-free, I flew to California.

I brought the cat home.

He outlived Aida's diagnosis. Six more years of that recalcitrant beast, as if stubbornness alone kept the tumor in his stomach at bay. A week after we slipped over the rim of the Pacific, into the golden land, I woke to the hiss of his labored breathing. His eyes were black lamps, undilated even in direct light, as if, greedy creature, he meant to drink in sufficient sunshine to make up for those lost years. He escaped as I was calling the vet. I'm sure his bones lie by ocean. He always knew what he wanted.

As do I, in this last season of my life. For me who once saw an end at twenty-nine, the years that have followed seem at times surreal, an unearned gift given to me on a mountain. I've seen the world change, if slowly, if not quite as expected. Take the city that was once Los Angeles. Its new name is an homage to a life-giving weed, its streets replanted with cacti and jacaranda trees that, every spring, drop purple blossoms. Mornings smell of dew, everyone recycling and monitoring air quality—but by noon there's a haze in the sky. Can't be helped, the scientists explain. For all the environmental protections enacted after ninety-eight percent of commercial crops and twelve percent of the human population perished in famine, there are qualities endemic to a place. The texture of wind. The cool ridge of the Santa Anas. The fact that this valley is a rough bowl into which all things come to settle. We obey our natures, in the end.

There were times I forgot, and fought mine. A midlife crisis of sorts found me on the explosion's ten-year anniversary. I canceled all restaurant pitches that day and holed up to watch a new documentary. More than one villain this time. All two hundred and ten were painted with the same crude brush, their fates declared proportionate to their crimes. My office door was locked and yet there entered, through the screen, meteorologist, heiress, the staff member who rocked the cat like a baby, and her. Their faces were followed by the name of the PAC that had funded the film. It was an election year, the Green Party campaigning furiously for higher taxes on the one percent, a cause I supported, as I told reporters. *But it wasn't exactly like that*, I tried to explain, *not all of them*, her name rising, clotted as cream. They cut and spliced my stammering until I was made a villain, too. After that, I stuck to yes and no.

Heartsick, I fell in love again. My lover was a PR strategist, an animal rights volunteer, and a new breed of evangelist, one of those who spoke with equal joy of God's love through prayer, and also peyote plants. She was young enough to have just missed the smog years, I half in awe of the crispness with which she saw the world in divisions of light and shadow, problem and solution. *The way to wash out your past*, she said, making it sound so simple, *is through acts of penance*.

At her urging, I turned from restaurant investments to philanthropy. My donations attracted press coverage, which led to diners flooding my restaurants and buying my lines of frozen foods, which led to money for more donations, more press, and so on till the private burden I'd thought to discard acquired a public life of its own. At first this made me uneasy. Sitting on panels with CEOs and venture capitalists who trumpeted the goodness of their philanthropy, and never their tax breaks or free publicity, I tried to feed nuance to audiences of politicians and donors, bankers and designers and housewives. Honesty left my listeners bored, or queasy. Eventually I learned to present my life as a neat moral package, wiped clean; as my clear-eyed lover pointed out, this was how fear of famine had been leveraged to pass climate legislation. It was the way of the world to make selflessness of selfishness, smooth pâtés from butchers' discards. No one paid to see blood on the plate. I went along. I even adopted my lover's ovo-lacto vegetarianism. But the day we broke up, I gorged myself on organ meats, my mouth singing with iron. My lover, with her clarion voice, became a congresswoman. I swore off love. And then, by accident, I became a mother.

———

I had my daughter on my own. For her sake, I looked, as I hadn't dared, into the future. Stepping from the doctor's office into spring day, I was suddenly conscious of the tender paper of my lungs, the velveteen spleen and liver, the fragile leaves, damp air, veins of my body that fed hers. For my daughter I banished instant noodles, cheap candy, nicotine, empty speeches, preservatives, hypocrisy; I disappeared from the public eye along with memories of the explosion. I spent the months of my pregnancy canning chokecherries and planting tomato vines that would vine into the next year of her nourishment, and the next, and the next. The ghost of the chef peered over my shoulder.

Quietly, under a new name I chose for myself and my daughter, I endowed a foundation for young women in the food industry. To run it I gathered the best of the chefs I'd met over the years, those whose plates were admirable, and everything that went into them too, kitchens and hires, farms and hands. They understood other kinds of nourishment: real chefs. Under their care the foundation would grow to dispense seed money, awards, commercial kitchen space, hot meals, education. Each day its auditorium rang with the voices of girls come for free classes on sustainability, and ethical business, and accounting, and the care of ecosystems that would ripple beneath the feet of my daughter, and girls like her to follow.

My daughter grew into her own tastes. From toddlerhood she'd push aside apples and fill her mouth with *Why*s. I understood what it was to both fear and admire your child the day she brought home an assignment on family histories. Obdurate, she pushed past my press clippings, my speechwritten talks, even my charming Parisian anecdotes. *That was so long ago*, I demurred when she came to rap at the tomb of the life I'd buried. *I was young and dumb. I didn't really understand what went on around me.* I'd named my daughter after no one; she was meant to be unburdened. *More intelligent people have weighed in on what happened. I have nothing to add, I hardly remember.*

I paused that night at my daughter's bedroom door. Her small face glowed, ghostly, in the light of the screen as she scrolled, article after article. I stood frozen at the threshold until her computer switched off. *Mom?* she said when I entered to say good night. *Can I ask you something?* I felt once more that vertigo, as if my heart lurched at the cliff's edge. She searched my face, grave. *Can we have pancakes for breakfast?* My answer seemed to satisfy her. I closed the door.

My daughter is independent, a scrape-kneed girl who moved so rapidly toward her ambition that I often failed to notice until she was already waving from the other side. At unexpected moments, her seriousness recalls my own mother, and then I tug her from her book or project, make her dance with me until she's laughing, annoyed. She got into her journalism program early decision, telling me only after her acceptance; if I felt a pang, I knew better than to ask that she live for me. So it wasn't for many years that there came a pause in her life's swift trajectory, a chance to take her on the trip she'd always asked for. To celebrate her new staff position at the *LA Times*, we traveled through Spain, Germany, France, Belgium. Italy, where I flinched from the continental light. I relaxed as we toured Neapolitan neighborhoods famous for the spiced calzones of their Syrian diasporas, and hiked stretches of Amalfi coast that listed, in addition to wildlife, the scientists and institutions credited with the revival of those species. This Italy was new to me. Safe.

And then one day, in Milan, my daughter brought an article to dinner.

She'd spent her afternoon at the national library. There, in the archives of a now-defunct local tabloid, was a piece dated to six months after my departure from the mountain. In salacious detail speckled with the occasional spelling error, the tabloid described the vehicular murder of a Milanese boy by a wealthy socialite. The boy's death had been instantaneous, the cover-up long. The article hinted at drugs and either child or canine trafficking, it wasn't clear. It alluded to a Japanese sushi chef.

This is the only mention of an accident, my daughter said. *There are no other sources I can ask. What really happened?* And then, *Okay, why are you laughing?*

I don't know what it was. Air or familiar sky, the rustle of olive trees around the restaurant terrace, or perhaps the sound of my daughter speaking with a boldness I'd always encouraged in her: an echo. As I looked out to the horizon, distance rendered the mountain both smaller and clearer, as time revealed Aida to be not only indomitable but a girl younger than my daughter, audacious and motherless and alone. Over bitten crusts and softened butter, the wine in my half-drunk glass shone like a beacon calling me to confession.

It's a very long story, I said.

I know.

My daughter had a confession of her own. All through Germany, and Spain, and Belgium and France, she'd been chasing the facts of the mountain. *It never made sense to me*, she admitted. *Even as a kid I recognized that the person I read about was nothing like* you, *they got it wrong. I've always wondered what else was wrong.* She took my hand. *Maybe I can get it right. Would you help me?* She looked at me across the table: me in my shawl and sensible shoes, me with my bare and tired face, me in my old woman's skin that rendered me increasingly invisible: she looked at me. At *me*.

Over hours and days, weeks of late nights, I chipped at the tomb around that year of my life. I had my daughter's help. Archives and private records opened to her credentials. She knew how to ask, without apology, for what she was not offered. Contracts and chronologies, personal papers and early drafts, brief mentions in unlikely sources. Nearly four decades later, I finally learned the name of the boy who'd died in Milan. In the public tax records that told a story of his family's poverty, I saw: my employer had never paid. My daughter tracked down the two siblings still living. She filled out the wire transfer. I remembered the precise amount spoken decades earlier, and asked that she adjust for inflation, for all else. *And bread*, I said. *Send bread, if you can.* When she raised an eyebrow, I told her the rest, too.

The rest. In cabs that sped through summer nights, over meals of pane carasau and white anchovies, through the clamor of a hundred voices that rose blaming and confessing and bragging and lying and contradicting and implicating and begging from the archives, I found myself telling my daughter about some of the voices that were missing. The staff member who could gut and clean a fish in seventeen seconds flat, and the one who'd rocked a cat like a baby. The song that shook the orchards as the field hands brought down fruit. Her voice. The tomb, pried open, was not full of dusty horrors. What emerged was vital enough to pound at my heart, that *rap-rap-rap*: it was still alive.

What do you think? I asked at the end, awaiting my daughter's verdict as I'd awaited that of mother, employer, jury, judge, cat, diners, voters, mobs, audiences, writers. She went to the window of the room that had grown stuffy. Opening us out to the almond trees, she said,

Given that your employer destroyed all records from the mountain, there are too many gaps. My honest opinion is that no one alive can get their arms around this story in a conclusive manner—to try would be irresponsible. That's the first thing I was taught. She saw my disappointment. *But if you want* my *opinion, not my journalistic one . . . I think you wouldn't be here without what happened. Which means I wouldn't be, either. Maybe that's selfish.* A shrug. *It makes me think she doesn't sound so awful. You know— she reminds me a little bit of me.*

At summer's end I kissed my daughter at the airport and turned north. Alone I followed the faint track of rumor up through foothills till each town held, at its small summit, a church. I came to a plain alive with the sound of cicadas. Shed husks littered the olive trees and yellow stones, but what seemed dead might also rise, vibrating. The cicadas' de-extinction remained a mystery: funded by no company for tax write-offs, credited to no lab employing protocols descended from a smuggled hard drive. Locals ascribed the miracle to a saint.

In the deep thrum of dusk, as insects called, insistent, for their mates, I remembered a day I'd turned my back so as not to see cicadas die. Three cycles of thirteen years had since passed. Then I'd believed her cruel, and careless, to release a creature without scripting its future. But had I looked, had I kept looking, had I cleaved to my faith—was hers not a faith of its own? In that church, in its own small altar, the saint's statue was worn so smooth it lacked eyes, a nose. Yet the depression of her mouth seemed to smirk.

She reminds me of me, my daughter said. And she reminds me of the girl who stands in class to outline a treatise on food waste; and she reminds me of the Youth Science Olympiad champion who describes, through pink braces, the video game she'll develop with her winnings, ships sailing through space to encounter small planets and strange creatures, no weapons on board, no matter of life or death; and she reminds me of the girl I see dancing at the bus stop, she misses a step, she stumbles, more joyful than skillful, her eyes are closed. She dances for herself. And she reminds me of those who fill the auditorium of the foundation I visit often now that my daughter is grown, girls young earnest prideful pretty angry plain uncertain ferocious dreamy skeptical who shape themselves as pastry chefs and caterers and molecular gastronomists, who might the next day decide to be, as well, butchers and picklers and practitioners of the arts of fried chicken, poetry, nanobiology. With the bewildering gift of life given me at twenty-nine, I've sown a little more fruitfulness through the world. In seed banks of Italy, in fields of Brittany where buckwheat waves high, in California forests seeded with sequoias so slow-growing that to plant them is an act of faith on the part of those who will never witness the fruit. There is time on this greener earth for girls to ripen into themselves; what they'll do with that is beyond anyone's knowing, seeing as they are not limited to anger versus dinner, seriousness versus sentiment, survival versus all life's rampancy. They can choose. She was cruel, and not, and cutting, and kind, and she gave, though not always to humanity, in her own unpredictable ways; I imagine her howling with laughter at the strangeness of how she's touched this world. She enjoyed a costume, and would gladly perform the roles of villain or saint as required, human judgment being of no concern. Her impatient gaze rose higher. And a stubborn mouth reminds me, and softness reminds me, and my daughter beaming on her wedding day reminds me as she says into my neck: *Thanks, Mom. You've done more than enough.* The tomb is open. I see her, and myself, all our possible selves in girls who step further into worlds beyond worlds beyond worlds. In the back of the auditorium I drowsed, believing this to be enough, my life already over, my name and face forgotten. And then one day, in the back of the auditorium, a girl asking about the land of milk and honey reminded me, and my heart leapt: stumbled: slows:

For forty-two seconds,

    I see the olive grove.

    I've slipped through.

    The trees are blooming, all of them, horizon to horizon a dull splendor.

How do you feel, asked the paramedics who restarted my heart. Over my body they called, *Time, one thirty. She was out for forty-two seconds.* I touched my chest, my stomach. *Hungry*, I said, and ate the crackers I was given, though they weren't quite what I wanted, nor the tender stems of my get-well bouquets, nor the mangos my daughter brought from her new home on a warmer ocean. The fruit sat fragrant in her lap as doctors explained that my condition was not unusual. For those who lived through smog, there was often this thickening in the walls of the heart, a tarry residue. The doctors paused. I asked if I could still eat mangos.

My daughter helped me home from the hospital. In my weakness I perceived the sturdiness of her. It was with the faintest tremor in her voice that she asked what I wanted to do with my remaining time. *I want*, I said, *to be a tree.* She thought it was the drugs speaking. I was asleep before I could share the secret I once learned of a pomegranate orchard's prodigious growth: Old trees, dying, may burst after fruitless years into sudden blossom, a final exuberance of flower and sugar. Toward sun. At the last, even trees ache in their sap for pleasure.

Beijing and Seoul I saved for January. When my daughter asked why not spring, why not when she and her husband could join, I told her I was keeping an old appointment. Was I sure? she asked, knowing the stroke leaves me fuzzy with dates, time become porous. *Yes,* I said. *Yes.*

The ash trees were leafless upon my arrival, the forsythia weeping black. I bought a baked yam in the shuddering cold and thanked the vendor despite our lack of shared language. I knew she understood. A part of the cook always makes it to the plate, sweat or curl of hair, desire or doubt, ambition or joy, and in that yam's salt crust I tasted her knowledge of loss. She dabbed tears from my face. Tried to sell me five more yams.

Every year left to me I will go in January to Beijing and Seoul. These hutongs are smoky from centuries of braziers, these hanoks flicking beams to the same unchanging sky. I wander past old stone walls soft with the oils of a billion billion hands. Once, I took my daughter to see an exhibition of a woolly mammoth. Stiff fur, dead gaze. Halfway through our tour the docent shut off the lights. In the darkness the mammoth lit up cool and blue. As I put my hand to my eyes my own skin blinded me. My hands, the bodies around me, each tile, each doorway: blue, as milk is blue. DNA is nearly impossible to destroy, the docent said. Traces remain through millennia. In certain lights, the past and present are indistinguishable.

Impossible, I might have said when I was young enough to think cynicism the mark of age, when life seemed one low gray corridor of doors swinging closed. Now past muddles present, caramel stirred through cream, and I see again that sky, that grass, that summer grove that seeded the long and fruitful life she gave me. There are worlds and worlds and worlds. I need only the one.

So often did I look for her across a crowded table when it is spring and green and we are young with the meat caught red between our teeth. Then our gazes have velocity. Then we slip from our seats, rooms, hours. At the edge of starfield she is waiting; she leaps. For so long I believed in her fall—

Clearer than ever do I see that other fall. Through grass, to soil, the sun turning to extravagance the earth's red dust. Her face above mine is dappled with the pleasure of tasting, being tasted. I've sampled this world in the years I was given and know, at the end, what was sweetest. The spice of loam. The sting of salt and sedge. The tongue, dumb beast, believes. I see her in a girl who stretches her arms through morning mist, in a crone whose rings flash beneath noonday sun, in a bing seller who in sunset's dying radiance hums as she pushes her cart home: a waltz. Now then again I would speed with her down the road all paths pour into, I would look into her face, all her faces, never away. Every year that remains to me I will walk the streets of Beijing, of Seoul. I look for a long, long time.

Acknowledgments

Appam at Gunpowder, Goa. Baby artichokes hand-picked by Chaz at Frank's Market, Seattle. Bill Clegg. Bing and da lu mian in my dad's kitchen. Biologists' chatter overheard at High Grounds Cafe, Iowa. *Blood, Bones & Butter* by Gabrielle Hamilton. Brandon Taylor. *Brideshead Revisited* by Evelyn Waugh. Buddig sliced turkey. Bun rieu at Mau, San Francisco. Burritos at The Hot Shop, Albany. Cabbage with pistachio milk at Mission Chinese, San Francisco. Cannelés at La Boulange, San Francisco. Capri indigos. Chicken McNuggets at McDonald's. Chili cheese fries at Wienerschnitzel, Salinas. Chip butties at The Trailer of Life, Cambridge. Chocolate pudding at KFC buffets. "CRISPR and the Splice to Survive" by Elizabeth Kolbert. "Demeter to Persephone" by Alicia Ostriker. *Dirt* by Bill Buford. "Dead Ringer" by Ben Calhoun, *This American Life*. Eggplant cookie at Gaggan, Bangkok. Fresh paneer at Dhamaka, New York. Fresh tofu at Sun Hing Lung, New York. Funghi alla griglia at Ristorante Pizzeria da Gianni, Calenzano. Grains and seeds at Atelier Crenn, San Francisco. Green onion slab at Acme Bread, Berkeley. Isaan sausages at Eathai, Bangkok. Jalea at Los Andes, Providence. "Japan's Rent-a-Family Industry" by Elif Batuman. Jian bing at the stall outside LinKeYuan, Beijing. Jojo potatoes from Safeway. Kare short rib at Musang, Seattle. Kat Chow. Mai Nardone. Mapo lasagna at Nightshade, Los Angeles. Mariya. Meng Jin. Muskmelon at Zakuro, Tokyo. *My Year of Rest and Relaxation* by Ottessa Moshfegh. Nic Baddour. Oden from 7-Elevens in Japan. Orange Julia from Plantworks, Seattle. *Out of the Silent Planet* by C. S. Lewis. Pear ciders in England. Pork chop at Nopa, San Francisco. Poularde de Bresse en vessie at L'Auberge du Pont de Collonges, Lyon. Prupisceddu in umidu cun tomatiga at La Ciccia, San Francisco. R. O. Kwon. Raven Leilani. Red Leicester from Sainsbury's. Riverhead Books, including Alison Fairbrother, Delia Taylor, Glory Anne Plata, Hannah Lopez, Jynne Dilling, Nora Alice Demick, Caitlin Noonan, Claire Vaccaro, Denise Boyd, Geoff Kloske, Grace Han, Jennifer Tait, and Melissa Solis. Rotisserie chicken from Costco. Sarah McGrath. Sarah Thankam Matthews. "Seeing Ershadi" by Nicole Krauss. Sesame chicken from Ranch 99. Shaokao in Ürümqi. Soleil Ho. Sour cream and cheddar Ruffles. Spit roast pineapple at Dinner by Heston Blumenthal, London. *Sweetbitter* by Stephanie Danler. The Clegg Agency, including Marion Duvert, Nik Slackman, and Simon Toop. *The Gastronomical Me* by M.F.K. Fisher. *The Lover* by Marguerite Duras. *The Red Parts* by Maggie Nelson. *The Sixth Extinction* by Elizabeth Kolbert. "The Third and Final Continent" by Jhumpa Lahiri. Tiger prawns at San Ramos, Lisbon. *Top Chef*, especially winners Melissa King and Mei Lin, and host Padma Lakshmi. Tortillas at Molino El Pujol, Mexico City. Toum and pita at Arabian Nights, San Francisco. Tudou si at Little Shen Yang, Union City. Tuna conserva salad at Pizzeria Delfina, San Francisco. Tuna niçoise sandwich at Bi-Rite Market, San Francisco. "What is the strangest thing that happened to you that you can't logically explain?" on r/AskReddit. Whole fish in all its forms. Wings at Brother Z's Wangs, Nashville. Zhajiang mian at my nainai's house in Beijing.

My family. Avinash and Kitsune. Spike and Bagu and every cat I've loved, however briefly.